A Simple Life

NEW YORK TIMES AND USA TODAY BESTSELLING AUTHOR

MELANIE MORELAND

A SIMPLE LIFE
by Melanie Moreland

MORELAND
BOOKS INC.

Edited by Silently Correcting Your Grammar
Proofreading by Sisters Get Lit.erary
Cover design by Feed Your Dreams Designs
Cover Photography by Adobe Stock/ Анастасія Стягайло

Cover content is for illustrative purposes only and any person depicted on the cover is a model.

Readers with concerns about content or subjects depicted can check out the content advisory on my website: https://melaniemoreland.com/extras/fan-suggestions/content-advisory/

DEDICATION

For Atlee. Enjoy the thrill of victory.

It happens only once.

JOHN

I heard Laura's truck pull up outside, the sound of her squealing brakes announcing her arrival. I rolled my eyes as I reached for another coffee mug. I needed to look at her brakes. Maybe her husband, Bob, and I could work on them this weekend. Now that the planting was done and the crops in, I had a little more time on my hands.

I snorted with amusement as I added cream to Laura's coffee. More time.

I wish.

The screen door banged open, and my nephew Cody rushed in. "Uncle J!"

"Hey, big man, careful with that door. It's old."

He laughed, not caring. "Can I get the eggs?"

I nodded. "You know where the basket is. And the deal. Every one you get and clean, you can sell and keep the money."

He grinned. "I know. But I have to save you six."

"Yep. Breakfast."

"Got it!"

He rushed past his mother, who was walking in, juggling her purse, a laptop bag, and a sack of groceries. I hurried forward, grabbing the sack and the laptop bag about to slip off her shoulder. "Stop being so stubborn and ask for help," I demanded, leaning down to buss her cheek. "And stop buying me groceries. I'm a grown man and can look after myself."

She chuckled and set down her purse, taking the bag from me. "I'm aware you can, but you don't. I saw the empty fridge when I was here on the weekend."

"I've been busy in the fields. Restocking is on the list."

"Well, I bought you a few days. And stop spoiling Cody. You don't have to pay him for chores."

"He's working toward a goal. I'm not going to miss some egg income," I chuckled dryly. "It teaches him."

She sighed. "You have always spoiled him."

"He's a good kid. He deserves it."

I watched affectionately as Laura unpacked and filled the fridge with the basics. My freezer was full, but during planting time, I did tend to forget to keep up with incidentals. I had lots of food, but most of it was frozen. It was a good thing the microwave and I were fast friends. In the winter months, I stocked up on premade meals so when I came in from the fields, tired, hot, and sweaty, I could pop in a bowl of stew or chili and let it heat as I showered.

But I had to admit, I appreciated the lunch meat, bread, cheese, and assortment of fruit and vegetables she placed on the shelves. I didn't need eggs or milk since my chickens and dairy cows supplied me with both. I bought my meat from local farmers, often trading my goods for theirs. During harvest, we all worked together in the community. Everything, down to the cheese I bought, was local and handmade.

I sat down as she finished, tucking her burlap sack into her laptop bag and pulling out her computer. "Down to business."

"Not a social call, then?" I asked dryly.

"I finished the tax files and the year-end." She slid a file my way. "Look them over, sign, and I'll submit."

"Got it."

"And I got an inquiry on 221. They're sending the application today."

"Oh, great. No viewing?"

"A friend of theirs—Cathy Rawlings from Mitchell— came and saw it. Said it would work well. I told her if they wanted to see it, they could tomorrow."

I scratched my chin. "The name is familiar."

"Used to be Cathy Jones. She married Bart and moved to Mitchell. The applicant is a friend of hers."

"Ah, explains it. So we have a reference."

She nodded. "They want fast possession."

"Great. It's empty, so that works."

She flipped through some papers as she sipped her coffee. "I renewed the leases on the other three properties. The house on Renfrew has another two years on their lease."

"Awesome. Satisfied customers."

She laughed. "Great little houses, well-kept, and decent rent. Why would they want to move?"

"That's my goal. I'm thinking of bidding on the old schoolhouse. Turning it into two apartments."

"Oh. Interesting concept."

I nodded, scratching my scruff thoughtfully. "I'll need planning permission. I'm going to put it forth at the next council meeting."

"Oh, speaking of which, Thelma's old diner has a new tenant."

My eyebrows shot up at that statement. Thelma Hopkins had run the local diner for as long as I could remember. She had passed away last year, and the building remained empty. She had been one of my mother's closest friends, and I had mourned her passing deeply.

"I thought the town council agreed to expand the drug store beside it."

"No, they decided to move down the street instead and take over that empty building. A new offer came forward, and they accepted it."

"Someone bought it?"

"Renting for the first while with an option to buy."

"Unusual."

Laura leaned back, sipping her coffee. "Unusual circumstances, John. Not a lot of people moving to Richton and wanting to risk opening a business."

"I offered to buy it."

"And keep it as an empty shrine to Thelma? We need another business in town to keep going forward. Not an empty building."

"I would have done something with it."

Laura laughed, running a hand over her head. "With what time? You are already stretched, John. This farm is huge."

"I have help."

"Which you need."

I inclined my head. My sister wasn't wrong. What had started out as a 500-acre farm was now 1700 acres. Corn and soybeans were my crops. Planting and harvesting them was a huge job, not to mention caring for them in between. But I loved it. Working the soil, watching the crops grow and flourish. Knowing the produce was the best in the region. My product was in demand, which kept money in the bank. The past few years had been good ones, and I was ready for the leaner ones that would follow. They always did.

My father had cautioned me to always be prepared. He hadn't been a farmer, but his father had, and he had taught both of us about fiscal responsibility. I'd spent a lot of time with Gramps, and he had left his farm to me. I'd never wanted to do anything else but work on the land. It brought me a sense of peace and completion nothing else could match.

My dad had run the local hardware supply store in town, and my mom had worked as a cook at the small hotel during the summer season and helped out in the store the rest of the time. Laura and I had grown up in a house filled with love, respect, and laughter. Not a lot of money, but there was always food on the table, clothes on our backs, and enough bounty to share. My grandfather had a huge garden that he gave the bulk of to my mother, who canned and preserved all fall. I still had the space out back and Laura helped, but we grew far less than we used to.

Laura was an accountant and a real estate agent. She looked after the renting of the five houses I owned in Richton. I bought them and, with Bob's help, fixed them up and rented them. I was a good landlord, keeping the places in tip-top shape. I had little to do with the tenants, Laura handling that side of the business for me. But when a repair needed doing, it was done right away. I rarely had an empty house for long, even in our little town. It was a great investment and a way to give back to the place where I'd grown up.

"Does 221 need any work?" I had been too busy to go check when the tenant moved out a few weeks ago. I hadn't expected it to rent again so quickly.

"Some trimming of the bushes. They've gotten a little overgrown."

"I'll do that on the weekend."

"A leaky faucet in the kitchen. A couple other small issues. I'll make you a list."

"Great. But nothing major?"

"A fresh coat of paint inside. But they requested that they could pick the colors and said they would paint. I said yes, but they had to be approved and that you would pay for the paint." Laura smiled. "The daughter likes pink, I understand."

"Ah."

I finished my coffee, stretching. A new family for the vacant house, the crops were in, and I had food. It was a good day.

"What sort of business is going into Thelma's? Another diner?"

"Sort of. A little more upscale than her sandwich shop."

I snorted. "That won't fly here."

"No, I think the concept is good. Open early for breakfast and lunch. Closes at 3:30. Simple fare, good coffee, and they have a hook I understand. Catchy."

"I liked Thelma's."

"You liked the meatloaf."

"It was the best."

"And her," Laura said softly. "You thought she was the best."

I looked over Laura's shoulder. I had been twenty-three, Laura eighteen, when our parents had died in a car accident. Their unexpected deaths had shocked us, leaving us both adrift for a while. Laura had already been dating Bob and he'd helped her through the rough times, but I was a loner and always had been. I had no one, and somehow, losing them had made me more introverted. Thelma had stepped in, becoming the mother figure I needed to keep me from totally losing myself in grief. She became my sounding board and confidante. Helped Laura plan her wedding. Was there when Cody was born. I saw her almost every day at her old-fashioned diner, and it was she who helped me stock my freezer in the long winter months, planning for the busy spring ahead. When she didn't wake up one morning, my life once again changed. Became darker. Lonelier.

"Sorry." I shook my head, realizing Laura had said something. "I was thinking about Thelma."

"I know you miss her, but she would be the first person to tell you to pull up your bootstraps. And to remind you this town needs eating places and new businesses. The prospective owner is twenty-eight and is enthusiastic. We need that. Try to be supportive."

"I will."

"Okay, great. Then you'll vote yes at the town council meeting."

"About what?"

"The new tenant wants some renovations done, and then there's the name of the diner."

"It's changing?"

"Of course it is."

"To what? The Sandwich Shop was a decent name."

She shook her head. "New place, new name."

"Which is?"

"Kind of a Big Dill."

"Say what now?"

"That's the hook. Something about pickles. It's cute, right?"

I snorted. "Cute. I hate cute. I'm not voting for that name."

"You're going to be outvoted. The business plan is solid, the money is available, and we have a new business in town. All pluses. Stop being grumpy, locked in some false sense of loyalty, and welcome the change, John."

Before I could respond, the door slammed open again, and Cody rushed in. "I got lots!"

I directed my attention at my nephew. "Good job. I hadn't had a chance today."

"Here's your six. Mom, you need to take me to Brennan's to sell these. And I need to go and help Dad. He's going to pay me to clean out the storeroom. I'll get that bike soon!"

I grinned. He'd been saving for a bike since before Christmas last year. Little did he know I had already bought it for him and he would get it for his eighth birthday in a couple of weeks. He could put his money in the bank and start saving. I'd been his age when I'd opened my first bank account.

"You going to the fair this afternoon?" I asked. Cody loved the spring fair. It was smaller than our summer harvest event but always fun. The kids loved the rides and all the junk food. The parents enjoyed being able to relax as the kids ran free. Everyone watched out for them, so they were safe.

"Yeah—I'm meeting my friends at four. Mom says I can have supper there."

Laura snorted. "I said you could eat. I don't think cotton candy and a corn dog constitutes dinner."

I laughed. "Let him be a kid, Laura. You did the same thing. Hell, we both did. We turned out all right."

She eyed me skeptically. "Well, I did," she drawled. "You should have eaten more cotton candy—maybe you wouldn't be such a grump."

"I'm not a grump. I'm quiet."

"And grumpy," Cody said with the honesty of a child. "But you're my favorite, Uncle J."

"Thanks, kid."

Laura stood and started stuffing files back into her bag. I slipped a twenty into Cody's pocket and winked. I wanted him to have a good time at the fair. He grinned and winked back.

"See you later, big man." I fist-bumped him, and he made an exploding sound, flicking his fingers wide like a bomb going off. "Don't give your dad a hard time."

"Nope!" he yelled over his shoulder, slamming out of the door again.

"I need to fix that."

"Get Bob to order a new one," Laura replied, starting to follow Cody. Bob now ran the large hardware place in town, having expanded it when he took it over. He managed it well, and it serviced several small towns around our area. He was also the local handyman, so he was constantly busy. We all were in our little town, often wearing more than one hat.

"I saw that, by the way," she informed me. "And you're not always a grump." She indicated the door Cody had run out of. "Never with him. Or me."

I shrugged. "You're different."

"Not everyone is her," she said quietly.

"I'm aware. But in general..." I let my words trail off, not wanting to discuss that subject. Or remember.

She smiled. "The rest of the world pisses you off, you mean."

I laughed. "Something like that."

Laura brushed off her skirt. "I hope that changes for you one day." She stopped before walking out. "Think about it, John. Stop resisting change. Try to move forward."

I didn't respond. Change and I weren't friends. In my thirty-four years, I'd learned every time there was change, it meant heartache.

I wasn't a fan.

And Kind of a Big Dill?

Not getting my vote.

2

JOHN

Early evening settled around me as I sat on my porch, the quiet of the night a peaceful balm. I rocked my foot slowly, letting the soothing movement of the chair settle the last of the uneasiness in my chest. I always felt that way when the past was mentioned. Whenever someone brought *her* up. I shook my head to dispel the thoughts. I refused to allow her to occupy space in my head.

I had a feeling Laura would inform me she lived rent-free there, destroying anything good.

I ran a hand through my hair, noting I needed to get a trim. I would go into town next week and get it cut.

I glanced in that direction, knowing, right now, the fair was happening. The Ferris wheel and Tilt-A-Whirl would be going nonstop. The air would be rife with the scent of deep-fried foods and sweet treats.

Families would be gathered, couples strolling, kids laughing. Glancing at my watch, I saw it was barely past eight. I could drive in, walk around, maybe have a corn dog. Chat with some neighbors and friends. It wasn't my usual style, at least not these days, but maybe Laura was right. I needed to move forward. Before I could overthink it, I had my keys in my hand, shutting the door firmly behind me, and climbed into my truck, heading into town.

Why, I had no idea, except I didn't want to be alone anymore.

The fairgrounds were busy, but I found a spot, parked, and headed toward the bright lights. Everything I recalled about the fair hit me. The sounds, the smells, the lights.

I wandered a bit, talked to a few shocked people, hid from some others I had no desire to converse with. I got a corn dog, munching on it as I walked. I watched the rides, a smile pulling on my mouth as I listened to the screams of laughter, a few shrieks of terror, and the general happiness around me. Deciding I needed a beer, I headed toward the tent, planning on getting a cold draft and sitting in the corner to watch people.

I skirted the main area, walking around a few passionate clinches, a couple arguing, and then headed toward my goal. But it was the sound of a scared voice that stopped me.

"No. Please, just leave me alone."

"Hey, darling," a slurred voice replied. "We just wanna have a little fun."

"I said no. Let me go."

Frowning, I stopped behind an enclosure, peering into the darkness. Three younger men were standing in a loose circle around a woman, who had her arms wrapped around her torso. I couldn't make out her features, but I heard the fear in her voice.

"I was just headed to the midway."

"You shouldn't have taken that shortcut," another of the men insisted. "We can help you have fun."

Rage simmered in my chest, and I curled my hands into fists. Stepping forward, I grabbed two of them by the shoulders, pushing them away from the woman.

"She said no. Are you fucking deaf?"

The two I pushed stumbled, falling on their asses. They blinked up at me, unsure where I had come from. In the dim light, I studied their features, but I didn't recognize any of them. I turned to the one still gripping the woman's arm. "Let her go. *Now*."

"Why don't you mind your own business?" he said, his bravado stupidly speaking up.

I stepped closer. "Why don't you remove your hands before I rip your arms out of their sockets for you?"

He blinked, looked at his friends, and dropped his hands. He stood back, holding them up. "Sorry, just a misunderstanding."

"You want to know another misunderstanding?" I snarled. "The lady said no. That means no. Here in Richton, we respect that word. And the law. I can see you boys aren't from around here, so I'll give you a choice. You have thirty seconds to get the hell out of here and never come back—or you can stay, and I'll take you all on. I'll even give you a head start." I chuckled, my voice low and threatening as I flexed my shoulders. "But I guarantee the only one standing will be me. I'll even help the sheriff pour your asses into the cruiser as he takes you to jail for accosting this lady."

"Jesus," one of the idiots still on the ground muttered. "I'm leaving."

In seconds, they had run off. I watched them with narrowed eyes, wondering if I should have called the police anyway. I turned to the woman, who was watching me with wide eyes.

"Are you okay?"

"Yes," she said with a nod. "They had just surrounded me when you showed up."

"I don't think they're from around here." I studied her. "Neither are you."

"No, I'm visiting."

"Ah."

"I shouldn't have cut through this area," she said. "It was unwise."

"You shouldn't have to worry about being accosted by drunken idiots at a town carnival," I replied. "But let's get you to the midway." I swept my arm out. "This way."

She went in front of me, and I tried not to notice the way her hips swayed. She wore a pair of loose denim overalls, but they didn't disguise her shapely form. She had a great ass.

I shook my head, clearing the thoughts.

She stumbled, and I automatically reached out, grasping her waist and pulling her close, keeping her upright.

For a moment, time seemed to stand still. She was soft in my embrace, her warm scent overriding all the other smells around us. Her hand clutched at my arm, the paleness of her skin contrasting with my much darker, tanned forearm. She fit under my chin perfectly, and somehow I knew if I lowered my head, her hair would be silky and thick on my cheek. Her breathing was shallow, her chest pumping the air quickly.

Surrounded as we were by the darkness, holding her felt oddly intimate.

And incredibly right.

I stepped back. "Careful, darlin'."

She nodded, and a moment later, we walked into the bright lights. She heaved a sigh and turned to look at me. It was the first time I could see her features clearly. She was pretty with dark hair and an unusual color of seafoam green eyes. They were framed by long lashes and were striking.

"Thank you," she said.

I nodded. "Good thing I was headed that way."

She looked confused, and I pointed to the right. "The beer garden. I was thirsty."

She looked over, then took in a deep breath. "May I buy you a beer?" she asked. "To say thanks."

My first instinct was to say no. But I found I didn't want to.

"Sure."

She smiled. Her full mouth curled into a wide, toothy grin, two deep dimples appearing high on her cheeks. "Great."

I took the beer she offered me, and we sat at a table in the back, sipping the cold brew and letting the chatter happen around us. A few curious gazes strayed our way, but I ignored them.

"I'm Quinn," she offered.

"John."

"Thank you, John."

I lifted my beer in a silent toast, grateful I had been there. I shuddered to think what might have happened. While Quinn was getting our beers, I had seen one of the local cops and told him what occurred, and he and the others were keeping their eyes open. He recalled seeing a trio hurrying through the parking area and a souped-up truck leaving quickly, and I had to agree with him it was probably them, leaving with their tails tucked between their legs.

He had shaken his head. "They were twigs compared to you, John. You could have snapped them like kindling. No doubt you scared the shit outta them."

"Good riddance," was my reply.

I looked across the table at Quinn. "You sure you're okay?"

"I'm fine." She leaned closer. "I assume you're a local?"

"Yep. Born and bred."

"I'm from Oshawa."

"And you're visiting a friend?"

She nodded. "My grandparents had a small place a few miles down the road. I came out in the summers. I met her when I was seven, and we've been friends ever since. We don't see much of each other, but I hope that changes."

I didn't ask how or why. I would never see this woman again, so I didn't want to delve.

I finished my beer, sliding the glass away. "Thanks for that, Quinn. Be careful, okay?"

She frowned. "Should I be worried?"

"No. It's normally a safe place. Just stick to the lighted areas."

She looked over my shoulder. "I might just go home."

The words were out before I could stop them. "I can walk around with you."

She paused, then smiled. "Great."

We strolled the midway, walking around families, couples, and other individuals. Most of the time, I walked behind her, a silent shadow. I didn't make eye contact with many people, not really wanting to talk to anyone. I had already done the circuit earlier, but something in me didn't want to leave Quinn alone. I felt an overwhelming sense of protectiveness for the woman, which surprised me. It wasn't normal for me to feel anything for anyone outside my family.

She was a talker, pointing out things I had never noticed before. How the lights glimmered in the dark. The sheen of the rides as they whizzed by. She noticed people's shoes, their hats, whispering in mock horror over the long talons teenage girls seemed to like these days.

"I would poke my eye out," she confessed.

I noticed her nails were short, buffed, and nude. I didn't tell her I preferred the natural look. It seemed too personal somehow.

But I did find her amusing, and I had to admit, her droll comments made me smile more than once. I couldn't recall smiling that much in a long time.

Quinn pointed out a few craft stands, and we stopped and watched the rides for a moment.

"Did you want to go on one?" I found myself asking.

"No. I just like to watch."

"Hungry?"

She laughed. "No. I'm good."

She stared at the game booths, laughing as a guy tried to win a teddy bear for his girl. She eyed me up. "I bet you could hit the bell."

"You want me to try?" I offered.

She hesitated. "Really?"

"Sure."

We joined the group in front, and I wondered how I'd gotten there. Standing in line, waiting to swing a mallet and win a stupid bear for a woman I didn't know. It was almost as if I wanted to impress her.

Inwardly, I scoffed at the idea.

At the head of the line, the ticket taker handed me the mallet. "Good luck."

I lifted my arms and swung, the weight almost hitting the top.

"Oh, so close!" he yelled.

Plunking down the money for another swing, I stepped back, sliding my hands to the end of the mallet and focusing all my energy. Again, I swung, this time the weight rushing up the post and hitting the bell loudly. The crowd cheered, and I let Quinn pick the bear. She opted for a pink one wearing a tutu. I felt something akin to pride as I handed it to her—like a warrior giving his queen the prize for winning the war. Which made me want to punch myself in the face for such a stupid thought.

She clapped, grinning, and her beauty in that moment stunned me. Her eyes glowed, her dark hair rippling over her shoulders. Her smile was incredible, the dimples deep divots in her cheeks. She glowed with happiness, and she hugged my arm as we walked away.

I felt the stirring of desire growing. The want to pull her into the shadows and kiss her so strong, I almost stumbled. I looked down, finding her eyes on mine. Time seemed to stand still as our gazes locked, the heat becoming a living, breathing thing between us.

Then her phone rang, breaking the spell. I stepped back, shocked to see how close I'd been standing next to her. I frowned as she answered, hearing the deep timbre of a man's voice. She furrowed her brow, turning her back. With the crowds around us, I couldn't hear what she was saying, but a dull feeling of anger rolled through my chest. A sense of déjà vu hit me.

Hanging up, she turned to face me. "I have to go. My daughter—"

I cut her off. "*Daughter*?"

"I have to go. He says—"

I had no interest in hearing what her husband or boyfriend had to say. Or why she had to leave. She shouldn't have been here in the first place, and I should have walked away when she offered to buy me a beer.

I turned and did exactly that.

3

QUINN

John disappeared into the crowd, gone before I could speak again. I had seen the horror on his face and heard the shock in his voice when he repeated "daughter."

He didn't give me a chance to explain. Instead, he had walked away.

And I didn't have time to run after him to try to make him understand.

I hurried to the parking lot, sticking to the lighted area and following a couple heading that way. I breathed a sigh of relief and locked the door, heading to Cathy's place. I shouldn't have listened to them when they told me to go wander the fair. To get out and clear my head. I should have stayed home. Been there when Abby woke up with a fever. Memories of my ex and his constant criticism about being a bad mother, a terrible wife, an overall failure of a human being played in my head, and I fought to shut them down. He was wrong.

Yet, as often as I told myself that, his ugly words occupied a place in my mind I couldn't seem to shut off.

I drove back to Cathy's, parking the car and hurrying inside. Cathy greeted me, laying a hand on my arm. "She's fine. I gave her some children's Tylenol and put a cold cloth on her head, and she's already cooler. She had some water and wasn't upset you weren't here. I told her you were running an errand." She smiled. "Go see her before she falls asleep." It was only then she noticed the teddy under my arm. "You got that at the fair?"

I nodded. "Long story. Jerk I thought was a nice guy. Ran for the hills when he found out I had a daughter. But the teddy will come in handy for Abby."

She rubbed my arm in sympathy. "Sorry."

"It's fine. Not like I was looking anyway."

I went past her into the guest room where we were staying. Abby was dozing, opening her eyes and gazing at me sleepily as I sat on the bed beside her.

"Hi, baby."

"Hi, Momma. Did you get your errand done?"

"Yeah. How are you feeling?"

"Better. I was hot and scared, but I'm okay now. Cathy was nice. And Bart gave me a popsicle. It tasted good."

"I'm glad. This might help too." I handed her the bear, the pink fuzzy animal making her smile.

"Oh, Momma, I love her!"

"I thought you might." As soon as I had seen the tutu and the sparkly necklace on the teddy, I knew it was the one I had to pick. I knew there was no doubt Abby was going to end up getting the bear, so I chose one I was sure she would love.

I checked her temperature, pleased to see it was almost normal again. When I had first left my husband, Abby had often woken up scared, her fever spiking. The doctor put it down to anxiety, and it had stopped not long after we were on our own. I should have expected it tonight. I shook my head, knowing I shouldn't have left her.

Lesson learned.

"Tomorrow, I'm going to take you and show you the town we're going to live in," I said quietly.

"Is it pretty?"

"It is," I assured her, brushing her hair back from her head. She loved a head rub. "Lots of trees and little houses. I saw a park and a playground. There's even a local swimming pool."

"Are we gonna live in an apartment?"

"No, a house. I put in an application."

"What's that?" she asked, her voice low as she began to drift.

"Like a questionnaire. They want to know about us so they can let us live there."

"Good thing we're nice," she mumbled.

I pressed a kiss to her forehead. "Good thing."

She fell asleep, her breathing deep and even. I watched her for a while, my thoughts racing.

For some reason, I couldn't get the jerk out of my head. How kind he'd been at first. His concern for my well-being. His low, rich voice. The way he made me feel safe by simply walking beside me.

I had felt something spark between us. I was certain of it. The warmth of his touch had held me captive.

Then I recalled his reaction to hearing I had a daughter.

I sighed. Single mothers weren't for everyone.

Even knights in shining armor who seemed wonderful.

I had learned my lesson that not everything was the way it looked.

It wasn't a lesson I was planning on repeating.

JOHN

The next morning, I woke up angry. I had been furious since I'd stormed away from the pretty Quinn at the fair. The pretty, *married* Quinn with a child. Hearing the deep male voice on the other end of the phone had hit me, my past playing out in a warped sort of replay. I had to leave before I did something I regretted. Although, the truth was, I already had. I should have walked away after helping her. Instead, I'd acted like an idiot, walking the fair with her, winning her a teddy bear like a lovestruck teenager.

I sighed as I poured a cup of coffee. At least I wouldn't be seeing her again. She was only visiting, and aside from a quick trip to the bank later, I had no plans on being anywhere I would run into her. I hoped her visit was a short one.

Draining my coffee, I set the cup in the sink and headed out to the fields. Some hard work and sweat would help clear my head.

I needed that.

Hours later, I stepped from the shower, running a towel over my torso and roughly drying my hair. I dressed in jeans and a shirt, rolling up the sleeves as I headed downstairs. My phone was ringing, and I answered my sister's call.

"Hey, Laura."

"Hi. Bob needs a favor."

"Sure."

"The delivery truck broke down in Mitchell. There's an order on it he really needs today. The store is still short-staffed, and I have three meetings—"

I interrupted her. "Not an issue. I'm headed to the bank, then I'll head to Mitchell and pick it up."

She sighed in relief. "I owe you."

"I'd accept dinner."

She laughed. "I should have known."

I chuckled. "Tonight is spaghetti night. I love your spaghetti." I paused. "And I want to give Cody his bike. There's a meetup in the park tomorrow, and I know he'd love to go."

"His birthday is soon," she admonished me. "But you're right, he'd love it, so go ahead. Not that I could stop you," she added.

"Nope."

"See you later."

The sun was high, shining in the cab of the truck as I drove back to Richton, the delivery Bob required in the back cab. I planned on dropping it off, loading up the bike, heading to Laura's place and surprising Cody. I would wait until his parents were both home to see his reaction, but I was excited to give him the bike. He was a good kid, and he deserved it.

Ahead, I saw an SUV pulled over on the shoulder, the hatch open. As I drove past, I saw the driver struggling to work on the flat. Unable to leave anyone, especially a woman, in distress on the side of the road, I pulled over, backing up. I swung myself out of the truck, heading to the vehicle.

"Hey," I called out. "Need a hand?"

She stood, a curtain of dark hair obscuring her face for a moment. Faded denim overalls hung loose on her, a plaid shirt underneath and sneakers on her feet making her look somehow smaller than I expected. Then she brushed her hair back, and our eyes locked. Familiar, striking seafoam met my blue, and instantly, the air between us grew taut with anger.

"You," I muttered.

"You," she responded, sounding aghast.

I bit back my question, asking where the hubby was. Instead, I swallowed.

"Need some help?"

"I can figure it out, thanks," she replied, sounding stiff and turning her back on me.

I watched her as she unsuccessfully tried to loosen the lug nuts. With a shake of my head, I went to my truck, grabbed the right tools, a can of WD-40, and returned.

"You'll be at that all day," I said.

"I've got it," she snapped.

"Yep. Looks like it. Don't be so stubborn."

When she ignored me, still trying to loosen the lug nuts, I bent and bodily lifted her out of the way, grasping her waist and moving her to the side.

"Hey," she protested.

I rolled my eyes. "Don't you have a sick kid you need to get home to?"

I bent down, spraying the rusty lug nuts and fitting the tire iron in place. "Or is hubs more the caregiver than you?" I added, my voice bitter.

She muttered something, but I ignored her, getting the lug nuts off and, with some effort, pulling the tire away from the wheel.

Quinn had managed to get the spare out, and I made short work of putting it in place and tightening the bolts. I tossed the flat in the hatch and turned to her.

"You shouldn't be driving on those tires. They need replacing. It could be dangerous. You're lucky it was just a flat." I warmed up to my argument. "Your city-slicker husband should be taking better care. Not letting you wander in a strange place alone. Letting you drive on bald tires. What if your kid had been in the car?"

She stepped closer, fury etched on her face. "First off, jackass, the tires are being replaced next week. Second, there is no husband. Why the hell would you jump to that conclusion? You think I'm the kind of woman who would flirt with a stranger if she was married?"

"Wouldn't be the first time," I snapped, even as I felt a strange sense of relief at the information she shared.

"It would be for me, you jerk."

Before I could respond, she glared and stepped back, no doubt to walk away. Except she slipped on the gravel and her leg jerked, her foot catching me on the shin. Between my jeans and lack of power behind the movement, it was like being bumped with a hard cushion. Her eyes grew round with horror, upset, no doubt, at the involuntary smack. Unable to stop myself, I grinned, which only seemed to fuel her fury. And for some reason, it made me want to make her angrier.

"Is that the best you got, sunshine? Try putting a little muscle behind it next time."

"It was an accident, but if I get the chance, I will." She glared at me. "You deserve a good, swift kick in the butt for your attitude."

"Well, given the way you kick, I won't change much."

"I don't think you *can* change, you grump."

For some reason, her words made me want to smile. Laura called me a grump all the time.

"For the right reason, maybe I could."

She rolled her eyes and began to walk away then turned around. "For the record, I am a single mother. The voice you heard on the phone was my friend's husband calling to tell me that Abby had woken up with a fever. His wife was looking after her, so he called." She shook her head. "But you didn't wait around to find that out, did you? You heard daughter and immediately assumed the worst." She slammed her hands on her hips. "Or was it simply hearing that I had a child that changed your mind? I know men hate knowing they wouldn't be number one in the relationship," she said scathingly.

"I like kids. What I don't like are cheaters."

"Then take up with my ex. And shame on you for assuming I was the one cheating."

I glared, the words out before I could stop them. "It's happened before," I growled.

"I'm not that sort of woman." She spun on her heel and stormed away. Her door slammed, and the gravel kicked up stones as she hit the gas, driving away in a cloud of dust.

I watched her go, feeling oddly unsettled. She was correct—I had jumped to conclusions when I heard the male tone of the call and then she said the word daughter. I never thought of any other possibility except I was being played again.

And now I was standing on the side of the road, unsure what to do next.

I sighed and headed to my truck.

It wasn't something I had to worry about. She was only visiting, and the chances of a third encounter were slim.

Right?

Cody finished off his second plate of spaghetti, draining his glass of milk, and wiping his mouth. I couldn't blame the kid. Laura made great spaghetti, and I had eaten three large plates myself.

Laura and Bob watched us, trying not to grin. They knew I was dying to give Cody his bike, and it was taking all I had in me to wait.

I sat back, casually laying my arm across the back of my chair.

"I got something in the truck I need help unloading, kid. You up to the task?"

He flexed his arms, no doubt thinking he looked tough and strong. "For sure."

"Great. I'll lift it, and you can help move it."

"Sure, Uncle J." He grinned, looking cheeky, and winked at me. "I won't even charge ya."

I laughed, and his parents rolled their eyes. We headed outside, Laura making sure that Cody stayed behind me. They stopped a short distance from the truck, and I reached over the cab, pushing away the tarp that covered the new bike. The rich blue gleamed in the evening sun, the light glancing off the chrome. With a grunt, I lifted it out, turning and setting it on the ground in front of Cody. For a moment, there was utter, stunned silence. He stared at the bike, his mouth open, unblinking. Shock was written all over his face. That gave way to disbelief, followed by pure, unabashed happiness. He looked at his mom, then his dad, then back at me.

"It's mine?"

"Happy birthday, Cody."

He was a blur as he rushed forward, flinging his arms around my waist and hugging me hard. I squeezed him back, the joy on his face all I needed. We spent the next ten minutes with him examining his new ride, pointing out every detail that thrilled him.

Which was a lot. I was surprised he took time to draw a breath.

Finally, I laughed. "Why don't you take it for a spin?"

He climbed on, exclaiming over another detail. "Uncle J—the paint changes color!"

"Yeah, I thought you'd like that."

"Uber cool," he enthused. "And BMX is exactly what I wanted! You upgraded the tires too!"

I chuckled at his enthusiasm. "I made sure it had everything on your wish list, kid. Plus, the helmet and safety gear. I expect you to wear it all."

He met my gaze, suddenly serious. "Thanks, Uncle J. You're the best. And I love it."

"Good. Take care of it."

"I will."

"Now, take it for a spin."

He grinned, pedaling away. Laura came beside me, looping her arm around my waist. "You made his year."

"He's a good kid."

She smiled up at me, her eyes glistening. "You're a good man."

The thought of seafoam green eyes glaring at me floated through my head. "At times," I said.

She shook her head. "The way you treat Cody is the real you. And one day, the right person will bring that out in you all the time. I know it."

I pressed a kiss to her head, having no words.

But again, Quinn came to mind.

I dismissed those thoughts.

Immediately.

4

JOHN

The next morning, I pulled up in front of the house Laura referred to as 221. She had a short name for all the houses I owned—either the number of the house or the street. I owned two houses on Ferguson, so using the house number was the easiest.

I was thoughtful as I walked the property, looking it over. Everything looked good, although I thought the eaves needed a cleaning. I could do that another time. Inside, I checked everything out, pleased to see how clean and neat the last tenant had left the place. Laura was right and the place needed a fresh coat of paint, but it was from usual wear. The new family moving in could paint it and make it their own. I checked out the tap and the few other items Laura had listed, taking my toolbox room to room and making the small repairs. I decided a new faucet was best for the kitchen, so I climbed into the truck and headed to the hardware store.

My brother-in-law was at the counter as I carried up the new faucet.

"Bob," I greeted him.

He grinned. "John."

"Playing cashier today? Hanging with the little people?"

He laughed, taking my ribbing easily. "Sonya called in sick. It's busy."

I looked around with a nod. "I can come help after I put in this new faucet if you need me to."

"Nah, we're good. Little man is in the back, cleaning his heart out."

"Still?"

"He's gonna keep saving." He leaned on the counter. "He rode that bike last night until his legs were too tired to hold him up. He washed and polished it this morning so he can show it off this afternoon," Bob said with a smile. "Laura's right—you spoil him. You're a great uncle."

"Don't let that shit get around. I have a reputation."

He winked. "Would never dream of it."

I took the faucet. "Later."

"Dinner tomorrow. Don't forget."

"Never."

I finished tightening down the new faucet, then opened the water lines and slid back under the sink to check for leaks. Satisfied there were none, I wiped at the dust I had created, then startled as a young voice broke the silence.

"Why are you in my house?"

I lifted my head, hitting it on the pipes. Cursing, I pulled myself out, meeting the eyes of a little girl. She was crouched down, staring at me, her eyes wide. I judged her to be about six, and she was cute, with her dark hair tied in pigtails and wearing a set of denim overalls with a frilly top under them. She looked vaguely familiar.

"You said a bad word!" she whispered.

I rubbed my head. "Sorry, Pumpkin," I murmured, the endearment somehow slipping out. "You scared me."

She giggled. "I'm just little. How could I scare you?

You're like a—" she paused, then smiled widely, showing off her uneven teeth "—a goliath!"

"That's a big word for a little girl," I mused.

"My momma teaches me words. She says they are im, ah, important."

"She's right."

I frowned as I noticed the bear tucked under her arm. A familiar pink teddy bear. Far too familiar. I swallowed at the sudden worry in my chest. "Who is your momma, and why are you in this house?"

"We live here."

"No, this is my house."

To my horror, her chin began to quiver. "No. Momma said this is our house. I picked my color and everything!" Then she jumped up and ran away, calling for her mother.

I stood wearily, running a hand through my hair when Laura appeared and my fear was solidified. I recognized the woman trailing behind my sister, now holding the little girl.

Quinn.

And judging from what her daughter had said, and the annoyed look on Laura's face, my new tenant.

"John?" Laura questioned. "What did you do?"

"He says we don't live here!" the girl cried.

I held up my hands. "I think a misunderstanding has happened. I thought I was alone, and this little one appeared and informed me she lived here." I fixed my sister with a look. "I wasn't expecting the new tenants so quickly."

Quinn stepped forward, meeting my gaze, hers direct.

Something in my chest kicked at the sight of her. Even though she was average height, I towered over her with my six-foot-three measurement. She wore denim overalls again, along with tennis shoes. Her daughter was dressed the same, although her shirt was pink and frilly, and Quinn's was another plaid one with the sleeves rolled up. They shared the same long, dark-colored hair. Their features were similar, but her daughter had darker eyes. Quinn glared at me, no doubt angry with me for upsetting her daughter. There was something incredibly sexy about her protective stance and the way she was willing to face off with me. Her pursed lips were full, and for some reason, I kept staring at them, wondering if they were as soft as they looked. An errant thought ran through my mind, curious to know what they would feel like against my own mouth.

I blinked to clear away those odd thoughts and briefly

wondered why I kept having them when I was around this woman.

"We didn't know anyone was here either," Laura informed me, giving me her own heated look that told me right now I wasn't a good guy. "Where's your truck?" she demanded.

I rubbed the back of my neck. "I drove to get the faucet, and it was such a nice day, I grabbed a coffee and walked back."

"Faucet?" Quinn asked.

I indicated the sink, feeling the need to explain. "Laura mentioned it was dripping, so I installed a new one."

She frowned. "So, *you're* the landlord?"

"Yes." I held out my hand, trying to be polite. "John Elliott." I formally introduced myself.

She hesitated, then loosened her hold on her daughter, and extended her hand to let me shake it. It felt small and cool under my touch, the skin smoother than my rough, work-worn hide.

"Quinn Harper."

I waited, and she shook her head. "And this is Abby."

"Hi, Abby."

"Momma, I thought he was a goliath. He's so big! And he called me Pumpkin."

I chuckled. "I'm sorry I upset you. You do live here— or at least, you will soon."

"So, I can have my color?" Abby held up a swatch, and I took it from her, the color a brilliant pink. I glanced at Laura, then back down at the bright tone. Normally, we stuck to neutral colors for the rentals, but it was only one room. I handed it back.

"Sure, Pumpkin. Great choice."

She squirmed out of her mother's arms. "I'm gonna go look, Momma! And I need to get Enid from the car so she can see our new room!" She held up the pink teddy. "This is my new friend, Fluffy. My momma gave him to me."

"Oh," I said, trying not to smirk. I looked at Quinn, who stared back. "And who is Enid?"

"Her favorite doll. I gave it to her when she was a baby. She takes it everywhere."

"And now she has a pink teddy. I saw one like it recently."

She ignored my little jibe. "She loves all stuffed things and dolls."

"Hmm." I didn't know anything about dolls or little girls. Laura had never been overly girly until she became a teenager. Then things changed. She discovered boys, and the entire dynamics exploded.

"They arrived early. I didn't think it was a problem letting them in a few days ahead of schedule. The house is empty," Laura explained.

"No, it's fine. A little warning might have been nice, though."

"I called and left you a voice mail, but I'm guessing you left your phone in the truck," Laura replied, her tone snarky.

I had. It had been an impulse to walk the short distance back to the house, and I'd forgotten about my phone. Technology and I were not close friends. I shrugged sheepishly. It seemed as if nothing I did today was correct.

"It's fine," I repeated, my voice coming out a little gruffer than I meant it to.

"We can pay a fee if you want," Quinn offered, lifting her chin.

"No need," I replied, annoyed. "I don't need a fee." I paused. "So, only you and your daughter?"

"Yes. I listed that on the agreement." She crossed her arms. "Is there a problem?" She glanced at Laura. "You never said there was an issue with a single mother renting the place."

Laura shook her head. "There isn't one. Right, John?"

I shut my eyes, feeling embarrassed. I hadn't read through the paperwork, or I would have known. And I wouldn't be making an ass of myself in front of this woman.

"Not an issue. Another mistake on my part." My voice was clipped. "I can help you unload a few things."

"I don't require any help, but thank you, Mr. Elliott."

I had a feeling I had just been dismissed.

I wiped my hands. "Fine. I'll be going, then. If you need anything, you have Laura's number."

And I walked out.

Back at the hardware store, Bob met my eyes, lifting his eyebrows and shaking his head. No doubt Laura had told him what an ass I had been to the new tenant. I waved him off and went to the back, checking on Cody. He was busy sweeping, the shelves tidy, a pile of garbage ready to head to the curb. He'd flattened and tied up all the boxes, and everything was in order.

I clapped him on the shoulder. "Good job."

He looked pleased. "I had been hoping to have enough money to get my bike before the town parade," he confessed. "A bunch of my friends are decorating their bikes to ride in it." He looked past me, then kept talking. "My old one didn't look so good, but I didn't want to say anything to Mom and Dad." He grinned widely. "Now I don't have to. And I get to show it off this afternoon at the park."

I felt a swell of pride for this kid. He was good-hearted and loved his parents. He didn't want to hurt their feelings. "What are you planning on doing with your hard-earned cash?"

"Mom's birthday is next month, so I'm gonna buy her something nice. And I'm going to put the rest in the bank. I want to mow some lawns and stuff this summer and make more."

I smiled as I ruffled his hair. "Sounds like a good plan, kid."

He stepped closer, his voice serious. "It's the best gift ever, Uncle J. Thanks again. I'll take good care of it."

"I know you will."

"Mom is gonna help me decorate it for the parade. I'm going with a jungle theme."

"Good choice."

I left him finishing his task, feeling proud. The kid made me smile.

My smile faded as I rounded the corner, spying Quinn and Abby at the counter, talking to Bob. I walked over, standing beside them. "Found a problem with the house?" I asked.

Quinn turned, focusing her beautiful eyes on me. "No. I was asking about the paint."

"Put it on the house tab," I instructed Bob.

"I can pay for the paint."

I huffed an impatient sigh. "I will pay for the paint and supplies. I would have if I'd painted the place. It's part of the service." Bob walked away, and I shook my head. "Stop being stubborn."

Her eyebrows flew up. "I beg your pardon?"

I leaned close. "Look, lady. I didn't mean to insult you yesterday. Or today. I certainly didn't mean to scare your daughter or infer there was a problem. Quit twisting my words and refusing help when it's offered."

"Is all the service you provide rude and demanding?"

"Only when someone pushes my buttons."

She stepped back. "I'm not pushing anything, Mr. Elliott. I think I prefer dealing with your sister."

"I prefer it as well."

"Good. Then we agree on something."

"Yes. Now, pick your paint and supplies, and let Bob or one of the staff carry them to your car. Surely that won't offend your independent attitude if it's not me doing the assisting."

Then for the second time that day, I walked away from Quinn Harper.

5

JOHN

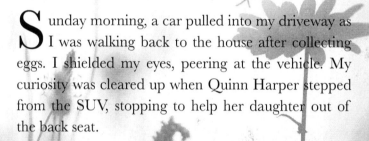

Sunday morning, a car pulled into my driveway as I was walking back to the house after collecting eggs. I shielded my eyes, peering at the vehicle. My curiosity was cleared up when Quinn Harper stepped from the SUV, stopping to help her daughter out of the back seat.

I frowned as she approached, wondering what she was doing here.

Abby ran up, excited. "Hi!"

"Hey, Pumpkin." I hunched down. "What are you doing here?" I asked, hoping by directing the question to her, I wouldn't say the wrong thing and ignite her mother's wrath.

"We had to bring your box!"

I stood, meeting Quinn's gaze. It was calm but wary. I was puzzled until she explained.

"You left your toolbox at the house."

"Oh. Sorry about that."

"I called Laura and offered to drop it off. I thought maybe we could clear the air."

I was surprised at her words. "Clear the air?"

She sighed. Before she could explain, Abby tugged at my pant leg.

"Are you a farmer?" she asked.

"Yep."

"Do you have horses and cows?"

I crouched down again. "I have chickens and cows. And lots and lots of plants."

"What kinds of plants?"

"Corn and soybeans."

"I like corn. Especially with butter."

I chuckled. "Me too."

"What are soybeans?" She looked at her mom. "Do you make soybeans?"

"They're used in foods, baby," Quinn explained.

"Like an ingredient. You love edamame. I make toasted soybeans for our salads."

"The crunchy things?"

Quinn smiled—a soft, warm smile that lit up her face. "Yes." Her expression did something to my insides, making me want to see it again. I shook my head at the strange thought.

I nodded. "They have lots of uses. They're used to feed animals, make things…"

"What sorts of things?"

I chuckled. Cody used to ask a thousand and one questions about everything.

"Oil, soy milk, tofu, all kinds of items."

"Cool. Can I see your chickens and cows, Farmer John?"

"Sure." I set down the basket I was carrying, feeling an odd jump of pleasure as Abby slipped her hand into mine. I showed her the chicken coop, and then we walked to the fence, where I lifted her up so she could watch the cows.

"Can I go closer?"

I glanced at Quinn, who nodded. I set Abby down on the other side of the fence, and she went closer to the small herd, who glanced at her with no interest and went back to chewing grass. She patted their hides, giggling, then raced over to the corner where some wildflowers grew.

"You're good with kids," Quinn said softly.

"When I'm not scaring them."

"Look, the past few days have been, ah, difficult. It was a long drive here. I was tired, anxious, and I wasn't myself."

I glanced her way. "You were attacked as well, darlin'." Why the endearment slipped out again, I had no idea, but I let it go.

"I was annoyed. They didn't hurt me, thanks to you."

"Still not a great introduction to the town you planned on living in."

She frowned, then shook her head. "Regardless, I shouldn't have jumped on you. And I was grateful for your help. I'm sorry I was rude."

Her words surprised me, and I turned to face her fully. "I apologize as well. There isn't a problem with you arriving early, and I don't care if there is a husband in the picture or not. Single mothers are incredibly strong, and I admire that. I wasn't offering to pay for the paint because of that, but because I take care of the houses I own. I want my tenants happy."

"Laura said the paint color Abby picked is usually not allowed."

I shrugged. "It's one room. It can be repainted when you move on."

She dug into her pocket and held up some swatches. "Are these okay?"

I glanced down and nodded. They were all soft neutrals. "Yep."

"Thank you." She paused. "I want to be a good tenant. I plan on staying here awhile. Building a life for Abby and myself."

The way she said the words, I had a feeling there was a story to be told. But I knew she didn't know me well enough to tell it, and I never got involved with tenants.

"I wish you all the best."

"Thank you. The next while will be busy, but I'm sure once I get things off the ground, it'll be great."

"Get things off the ground?"

She nodded. "I'm opening the new restaurant in town."

I stared at her. "Where the Sandwich Shop was?"

"Yes."

"You're the dill idea lady?"

"Yes." She narrowed her eyes, putting her hands on her hips. "You have a problem with that?"

"Kinda a silly name. Nothing wrong with Sandwich Shop."

"That's the old name. This is a new place with a new name. And it's not silly, it's catchy."

I snorted. "Such a city slicker. We like it simple around here."

She called to her daughter. "Abby—we have to go. Come on!" Then she turned to me. "Maybe they keep it simple so farmers like you can understand."

"Farmers like me?" I asked, stepping closer. "You think I'm simple?"

"I think you're rude and closed-minded." She shook her head. "I came here to apologize and start fresh, but I see that was a mistake."

"Obviously." I waved my hand. "Name your restaurant whatever you want. Hell will freeze over before I eat there."

"You...*ass*," she hissed.

Abby crawled through the fence. "Why do we hafta go, Momma? I like it here!"

Quinn grabbed her hand. "Too many animals here, Abby. Rude, bad-mannered animals."

She flounced away, and I watched as she got to the vehicle, struggling to lift the toolbox from the back. She tossed it on the ground, the lid popping open and tools spilling out.

"Whoops," she called. "Sorry, city slickers don't know how to care for farmer tools."

And she drove off. I was pretty sure she flipped me the finger as she did.

I turned and looked at the cows.

"Well, that went well."

Monday evening, I pulled up to the small town hall, sliding out of my truck as another vehicle parked beside me. Quinn stepped from the driver's side, and our gazes met over the short span separating us.

"Here to vote against my name, Mr. Elliott?"

"I have plans up for a new renovation on an old building."

"I looked around today. It seems you own every house available for rent here."

"Moving already?" I asked mildly.

"I thought perhaps it might be for the best."

"There are a few places in Terryville. I don't own those. Not as nice, though." I slammed my door and stepped closer. "You don't have to move. We don't have to like each other for you to rent a house. I won't bother you."

She frowned, her shoulders slumping. "That's the problem, Mr. Elliott. For a few moments these past couple of days, I did like you."

I was at a loss for words. I had liked her too. Then I opened my mouth and stuck my foot in it. But I didn't want to drive her away.

"Don't move, Quinn. Abby picked her color," I said quietly. "If you have any issues, call Laura, and they will be addressed immediately. I give you my word."

She hesitated, and something passed between us. A silent conversation—a promise given, one accepted. We would agree to disagree and be strangers who lived in the same town.

It was for the best since we seemed to strike sparks. Yet I had to admit, a small part of me felt sad at the thought of the distance we would keep.

She walked away and I followed, sitting on opposite sides of the small room. My request for the renovations came up, I answered some questions, and I was granted permission to move ahead. I sat down, half listening to the few items on the agenda.

My ears perked up at the sound of the request for the new name for Thelma's old place. There were a few remarks, some laughter, and the mayor smiled at Quinn. "Unique idea."

She stood. "I make pickles. Really good dill pickles—my grandmother's recipe. Each sandwich or plate comes with one. Hence the name." She met my eyes across the room. "Some find it silly. I think it's perfect."

Mayor Rhodes chuckled again. "Normally, this is not needed, but since you are on a trial run here, we want to make sure no one objects to the name." He glanced around the room.

I knew if I held up my hand, I could make it more difficult. If more than one resident objected, they could ask Quinn to change the name. I glanced her way, noting the stress showing in her expression, the way she was holding her shoulders. This meant a lot to her.

Beside me, Laura squeezed my hand, and I squeezed back in silent acknowledgment.

Laura was right. It was time to move forward. I couldn't do that to Quinn.

"Sounds kinda cute," I offered.

Quinn's head snapped in my direction, shock on her

face. A few other people murmured their assent, and when old man Harvey grumped, I shook my head.

"Come on, Harvey, what's not to like about pickles?" I called over.

He laughed, and a moment later, Quinn had her name.

Laura beamed at me. "Good job."

I waved her off. "Just making sure I get my rent."

She shook her head. "Keep telling yourself that, big brother."

A few moments later, I headed to the truck, tired, hungry, and wanting to be alone. Hearing my name being called, I turned, seeing Quinn hurrying after me. She stopped in front of me, confused.

"Why?" she asked.

I shrugged. "It's a name. In the end, that's all it is. You want to name your restaurant after a pickled vegetable? That's your business."

"Thank you."

I turned to leave, and she reached out, grabbing my hand. I looked down to where she was touching me, then back at her. The sudden desire to hold her hand, pull her to me, was as surprising as it was shocking.

"Maybe hell will freeze over sooner than you think," she whispered.

I shook my head, not able to explain to her my reasons.

"I do wish you luck, Quinn." I pulled my hand back. "Take care."

QUINN

I slid some freshly laundered towels into the linen closet with a sigh. I walked into the kitchen, somehow the memory of finding John there a few days ago flickering through my mind. When Laura had shown me the house, I knew it was perfect for Abby and me. Small but well cared for, it had a nice yard, even a porch where I could sit and watch her play. Two bedrooms, a good-sized kitchen, and a cozy living room with an electric fireplace made it homey. The floors were hardwood and gleamed with well-worn age. The appliances were still fairly new, and the place even had a stacking washer and dryer, which was a bonus. The yard was well-kept and not overly large, so I could look after it easily. The fence was in great shape—actually, everything was.

Modest, cozy, and simple. A far cry from the huge, rambling house we left behind. The expensive cars. The complicated life I tried so hard to find my place in. The constant failure my ex liked to remind me I was—at least in his eyes.

I poured myself a small glass of wine and wandered into the living room. I sat on the sofa, running my hand along the soft fabric. No more cold leather. No sterile environment that was showroom-perfect. Instead, the furniture was homey. Not expensive, but comfortable. A rug I found at a secondhand store was warm under my feet. The chair I had bought there as well was worn but snug. Some of Abby's toys were in the corner. I already felt more at home there than I had in my entire marriage.

I had painted the living room and the hallway, enjoying the task. The walls were a soft bisque color. I planned on using the same neutral in the kitchen, and I had a warm sage green for my room, but I would do it last.

A noise from Abby's room caught my attention, and I went down the hall to check on her. She was asleep, the sound I heard simply a dream muttering and not an upset one. I tucked her leg in, brushing her hair back from her face. I picked up a couple of toys, placing them in the toy chest. I had painted her room first, the bright pink making her so happy. I let her pick her furniture, and the white canopy bed and dresser looked nice in the space. I'd added a fluffy rug, and she chose some frilly curtains and a bedspread in a checked pink-and-white that she loved. The room was bright, girly, and fun.

Again, a direct contrast to the bland white space she'd lived in the past few years. I was doing the opposite of everything we had known. Everything we had both hated and been forced to live with.

I bent and pressed a kiss to Abby's head. She gave me the strength to wake up every day and move forward.

I returned to the living room, picking up my wine and sipping it. Tomorrow, I would be going to the restaurant to check on the progress there. I hoped to open in a couple of weeks if everything went according to plan. Luckily, the kitchen was usable and spotless—the last owner a local, beloved member of the community. I was reusing a lot of the things left in the kitchen. The front of the restaurant was getting fresh paint, new tables, plants, and other updates, but I was sticking to my budget.

When Cathy had told me about the opportunity, I knew I had to take it. We needed a new start. A fresh place where my ex had no influence and would never come looking for us. I loved the small town, recalling the summers spent with my grandparents. The chance to build a business that would keep me busy and use the talents I had been forced to put aside during my marriage.

The fact that I knew Preston would consider the investment foolish and running a restaurant low-class only added to the appeal. His opinion didn't matter anymore, but I had no doubt he would find out and be scandalized. I had to admit, the thought of his reaction made me giddy. He would hate it since he could no longer order me around.

Finding this little house was the icing on the cake. I loved the brightness, with the big windows, the massive oak tree in the front yard, the peacefulness of the neighborhood, and the friendly people.

Well, mostly friendly.

John Elliott came to mind. Or Farmer John, as Abby referred to him. I thought of the man who had stepped in and saved me. His size had struck me first. He was tall, broad, and powerful, and his muscles had muscles—no doubt from the daily physical work. His blue eyes were intelligent and shrewd. Kind at times, angry in other moments. Yet, somehow in all instances, they held a hint of sadness and even a vulnerability I knew he would hate anyone to see. His hair was a light brown, the ends bleached from the sun. He was rugged and masculine, nothing about him soft.

Except his smile when he directed it at Abby. And, for a few wonderful moments, at me. When his low voice uttered the word "darlin'."

But that changed quickly. We were oil and water—never mixing. He was quick to think the worst of me, and I was too fast to insult him.

But I was grateful he allowed me to rent this place and he hadn't made my life harder by objecting to the name of the diner.

Even if we were never more than landlord and tenant, I could live with that.

But I had to admit, the thought made me sad.

Which was silly.

I had to put that and the thought of him out of my mind.

JOHN

I stepped out of the hardware store, staring across the street, cursing under my breath. The sign *Kind of a Big Dill* hung over the sidewalk, the silly name making me shake my head. Everyone thought it amusing.

Except me. I didn't vote against it, though. Somehow I couldn't bring myself to hurt Quinn that way.

I had to admit, though, I missed the simple *Sandwich Shop* that had hung there ever since I was a kid. I missed Thelma Hopkins.

If I was honest, one of the reasons I missed her was because my relationship with her was a lot less complicated than the one I danced around with the new owner, Quinn.

In the month since her restaurant had opened, we had bumped into each other several times. It was odd since every time we did, I knew she was close even before our eyes would clash. The unusual seafoam color of her gaze always caught me off guard. So did the intense awareness of sensing her. I didn't understand it.

She was always unfailingly polite, greeting me with a smile and a friendly hello. Invariably, I said something wrong and those eyes would flash, but her smile never faded. She often muttered curses or names under her breath, but to anyone looking, they would simply see two people exchanging pleasantries. They had no idea of the constant war between us. I had managed to insult her wardrobe, shoes, restaurant, even the way she had trimmed the front bushes at the house. My foot was constantly in my mouth, and I had taken to avoiding her if possible.

I threw the seed and the new rake in the back of my truck, gripping the sides of the cargo walls. My stomach was grumbling loudly. I had been snappy in the hardware store, acting, as my nephew would call it, "hangry."

I had been so busy all day, I hadn't eaten. I didn't want to go to the modest Chinese place, the pizza parlor, or the more upscale Golden Butter restaurant in our small town. And the coffee shop didn't serve meals, leaving only Kind of a Big Dill.

And Quinn Harper.

The bane of my existence.

If I went in to eat and she saw me, she'd be all smiles, sweetness, and light. And no doubt crowing in delight at her victory. I'd sworn I would never eat there. A stupid thing to say, but as I realized, I often said stupid things to Quinn.

Everyone loved her. Proclaimed her the best thing that could have happened to Richton.

She was nothing but a pain in my ass, and I refused to succumb to her charms.

If I did, the slope that would put me on was too slippery, and winter would close in fast.

My stomach grumbled again, making up my mind. It was either eat something across the street in enemy territory or do my needed grocery shopping then drive back to the farm and fix myself something to eat.

By then, I'd be past hangry and downright miserable.

The choice was made for me as I felt another rumble pass through me.

Eat.

I crossed the street, my stomping feet indicating my mood. I opened the door and stepped in, surprised to see it fairly busy for this time of day. Some tables were taken, a couple of locals at the counter. I had to admit, it smelled good. Not meeting anyone's gaze or looking too closely, I sat in the end booth at the back, grabbing a menu. The kitchen door swung open, and I let out a sigh of relief when Tammy Becker walked out, carrying a tray. I'd gone to school with her brother. She was a lot younger than us, so I had known her all her life. She was perky, pretty, and kind. Engaged to be married next month. She delivered some food, crossing over to my booth with a smile and the coffeepot in hand.

"John Elliott, how are you?" she asked, filling the mug already on the table without asking.

"Good, Tammy. Hungry."

She laughed, indicating the board behind her. "You came to the right place. The special platter today is delicious. And big. It might even fill you up."

I glanced at the board and nodded. "Sounds good. Fast, if you can. I got a ton of work waiting."

"Not a problem. Cheese on that sandwich?"

"Yep. Everything."

"Got it."

She walked away, and I relaxed. Maybe Quinn was out. Busy somewhere else. I could eat and leave. Pay cash. She'd never even know I was here.

It was for the best. Every time we met, there were sparks. I acted badly, she smiled sweetly, and I stormed away.

It was sort of our thing.

Not that we had a thing.

Quinn Harper meant nothing to me.

She owned a local business and rented a house from me. That was it.

I didn't care that she was a single mother.

I never noticed how pretty her dark brown hair was. How it contrasted with those seafoam green eyes of hers.

Never.

And I certainly didn't fantasize about that mouth of hers. Silencing it with my own or seeing it wrapped around—

"Hi, Farmer John!"

I startled at the sight of the little girl now sitting across from me in my booth. She clutched a doll in one hand and a cookie in the other. She was a replica of her mother, right down to the sweet smile and the stubborn temperament.

And unfailingly irresistible.

"Hey, Pumpkin."

She grinned, her teeth uneven and crooked, missing a couple in places. It gave her an impish look. She wore overalls, paired today with a plaid shirt. I knew without looking there would be sneakers on her feet.

Again, just like her mother.

"What ya doing?" Abby asked.

Tammy appeared, sliding a huge plate in front of me. Steam drifted off the soup, and the sandwich and fries looked delicious. My mouth watered, and I forgot all the reasons I was against this place and could only see the one right thing.

Lunch.

"Eating lunch," I responded, picking up the thick roast beef sandwich and taking a bite. I chewed slowly, the tender meat and cheese tasty. The horseradish tickled my nose, and I almost groaned at the taste.

"Are you gonna eat all that?" Abby asked in wonder.

"Yep." I held out a French fry. "You want one?"

She grinned. "They're my favorite. Momma only lets me have them every so often."

"Oh yeah?" I turned my plate, pushing it closer and adding more ketchup to the side. "Help yourself."

There was silence for a few moments as I ate, the food dispelling the slight headache and feelings of discontent that had been forming. I took a bite of the large pickle on the plate, surprised at how delicious it was. I knew the catch of the place was every sandwich came with a huge homemade dill pickle, hence the silly name. And now that I had tried it, I had to admit, it wasn't a bad idea. I stood by my thought that the name was ridiculous, though.

The soup was rich and thick with vegetables. I was enjoying it all, even the quiet company of Quinn's little girl, when she spoke. She had taken a few of the fries, dipping them several times in the ketchup, licking it off her fingers. She was polite, not greedy, and she had good manners.

"Do you like my momma's pickles? I help make them!"

"They're really good," I assured her.

She leaned close. "Are you gonna order dessert, Farmer John?"

I had to smile at her nickname. She had called me that since the day she'd come to the farm with her mother to return my toolbox.

It had been an unmitigated disaster.

"Maybe. Any suggestions?"

"The chocolate cake with cherry ice cream is the best."

"Is that your favorite?"

She nodded.

"Does your momma only let you have it every so often?"

Again, she nodded, eating a French fry smothered in ketchup.

I got Tammy's attention, ordering the chocolate cake and cherry ice cream.

I looked around, no longer hungry, but curious.

Where was Abby's mother? Did she leave her here to be looked after often?

The cake plate and extra fork arrived in front of me, and I slid the plate closer to Abby. "Help yourself," I said again. We shared the cake and ice cream, and I watched with amusement as she took the last bite of the ice cream, her cheeks full.

Then her eyes grew wide, and I tried not to smile as she chewed fast, swallowing.

"Brain freeze?" I guessed.

She blew out a long breath of air, and I began to laugh. I couldn't help it. She looked adorable and sweet.

Then I felt it. That tingle that happened every time Quinn was close. I turned my head to see her standing at the end of the booth, watching us. Her eyes were narrowed, her hand on her hip. I tried not to notice she wasn't in overalls and a flannel shirt today. She wore a dress. One that touched at her breasts, hips, and swirled above her dimpled knees.

Why the hell did her knees have to have dimples?

She crossed her arms, pushing her breasts together.

Had they always been so…bountiful?

"Farmer John," she greeted me. "You're not really letting my daughter eat your cake, are you?"

"He gave me French fries too, Momma!"

Her eyes narrowed more. "He did, did he?"

"Yes—he told me to help myself, so I did."

I turned my head, trying to silently warn Abby to be quiet. But she was smiling and happy, pleased to see her mother, not holding anything back.

"Farmer John isn't a grouch like you say, Momma. He's been really nice!"

It was my turn to glare at Quinn.

"I was being nice because she seemed to be alone. You use your new business as a babysitting service, Quinn?"

"Go in the kitchen, baby, and I'll be there soon. We'll make some more cookies."

Abby slid from the booth, stopping. "Thanks, Farmer John. I had fun." She moved a little closer. "I hope you're not in trouble."

I met her eyes, shaking my head. "It's all good, Pumpkin."

She scampered away. Quinn slid into the booth in the spot Abby had vacated. For some reason, her closeness made me nervous, and I knocked over my glass of water as I reached for it. It was almost empty, but a little spilled over the edge of the booth.

"Shit," I cursed.

"Leave it. I'll get the mop in a moment. I want to clear up your misconception first."

I met her eyes.

Big mistake.

The seafoam green was like the ocean in a storm. Turbulent and angry.

"My daughter is my number one priority. Always. I had an appointment with the doctor and the insurance company, and my babysitter got sick. I had no choice but to either cancel the appointments or leave her here. For the first and only time. Tammy was watching her. I'm sorry if she bothered you. Since I didn't know that hell had indeed frozen over, I wasn't expecting you to be in here today. And I certainly didn't expect to find you sharing your lunch with her. I assure you she is well-fed." She took in a deep breath. "Consider your lunch on the house."

"You were at the doctor? Are you okay?" I asked, ignoring the rest of her speech and concentrating on those words.

"I'm fine." She waved her hands. "I slipped and jarred my hip."

Tammy walked past. "And burned her arm on the grill."

Without thinking, I lifted Quinn's arm, inspecting the gauze-covered patch on her forearm. "You need to be more careful."

"It was an accident, which rarely happens. You need to relax, Farmer John."

"I'm plenty relaxed."

She shook her head. "Two miracles today. You in here, and you smiling." She regarded me as she slipped from the booth. "You're very handsome when you smile."

Her words caught me off guard, and I found myself sliding from the booth, standing close to her. "You shouldn't say things like that."

She shrugged. "I say what I see. You don't smile very often, but you do when Abby is around."

I dug my hand into my pocket. "I like her. And I'm paying for my lunch. I enjoyed my time with Abby. She ate a few fries and a couple bites of cake. No big deal."

"You made her day."

I shrugged.

"You're very kind under all that bark, aren't you?"

"Hardly."

She smiled in disbelief and began to back away. Her foot caught on the water I had spilled, and with a gasp, she began to fall backward. I lunged forward, catching her and dragging her against my chest.

She stared up at me, startled. I gaped down at her, the sensation of holding her seeming extraordinarily right. The world stopped moving for a moment as our gazes held. Slowly, I stood, still holding her in my arms. I shook my head to clear it. "You're an accident waiting to happen," I growled, knowing I needed to step back. Move away from her.

I regretted my words as soon as they were out. Still, she smiled. That soft, gentle smile that did something to my chest.

I hated it.

"You saved me. Again."

I stepped away, shaking my head. "Don't read anything into it. It was my fault I spilled the water. Wouldn't want you suing me or anything."

"Thank you."

She tilted her head, then rose on her tiptoes, placing her hand on my arm. I realized she was going to kiss my cheek. Instead of backing away, I turned my head so our mouths met.

Gently.

Sweetly.

It was as if a volcano erupted inside me, setting every nerve ending on fire. Desire tore through me. Longing that I had never experienced until now burst forth.

I jerked back, shocked.

I wanted her mouth back.

I wanted to yank her into my arms and kiss her until she was breathless.

Until she felt the same passion I was feeling.

Somehow, I found the strength to move away from her totally. I gazed down at her. Saw something I hadn't noticed in those beautiful eyes before.

A quiet yearning.

One I didn't dare address.

I flung some money on the table and rushed away before I gave in to my impulse and wrapped her in my arms again.

I hurried to my truck and drove away like the hounds of hell were pursuing me, one thought repeating itself in my head.

I had kissed her. Quinn. The woman who irritated me beyond anything else.

I had *kissed* her.

And I liked it.

Dammit.

7

JOHN

I sat on the porch, beer in hand, watching the sun sink low, the colors around it vivid. I enjoyed our sunsets, seeing the way the sky changed and darkened. Watching the light glint off the fields and pond in the distance. It was peaceful and calm.

Unlike my chaotic thoughts.

Since I had run from Quinn, she was all I could think about. The feel of her mouth underneath mine. How it felt to hold her. The all-too-brief encounter played on repeat in my head, no matter how much I tried to block it out.

The sound of a car approaching interrupted my musings, and I watched as Laura pulled up and walked over to join me on the porch, sitting in the other rocker.

"Hey," I greeted her.

"Hi." She looked at the beer in my hand. "You got more of those?"

"Yep." I pushed the little cooler I kept outside toward her with my foot. "Help yourself."

She chuckled and took one, taking a long drink, then resting her head back.

"You okay?" I asked.

"Yeah. Just been a day. I have a new client wanting to buy a house, and she is leading me on a merry chase. I don't think I'll find her what she wants." She paused, taking another sip. "I don't think anyone can."

"Ah, one of those."

She nodded. "I'm her fourth real estate agent."

I blew out a long whistle. "How many towns had she looked in?"

"Six, so far. She's from Toronto. Thinks she wants to live in a charming, small town." Laura made air quotes as she spoke. "But the reality is, she wants the impossible. A huge house with all the modern features, but not new. Small town, but all the conveniences of a big city. Today, she asked me if there was a way of containing the number of fields and cows around here. She suggested that a Costco would be a good investment for the locals."

I chuckled. "She'll figure it out eventually."

"In the meanwhile, she's wasting my time. I'm going to suggest she look up north."

"Good plan."

We rocked and sipped in silence for a few moments. "Where's Cody?"

"Off riding with his friends, then a sleepover at his buddy Mark's place. Bob's on the sofa watching a baseball game. Or so he says. I heard snoring before I left."

"I see."

"I went past 221 earlier."

I tensed. "Problem?"

"No. But I noticed Quinn outside looking at the oak tree. I stopped to chat with her. She wants to put a swing on it for Abby. Nothing fancy, just a simple swing. Apparently Quinn used to have one at her grandparents' and loved it. She asked if she could have permission."

"I don't see a problem, but she needs to make sure it's safe." I frowned. "I don't think building things is in her playbook."

"I think she'll hire someone."

I grunted. "I could do it. I've got the perfect piece of wood. Add some sturdy rope, and it would be safe for Abby."

Laura was quiet for a moment. "I don't think she's comfortable asking you. I get the feeling you two don't get along."

I snorted in derision. "If you mean I'm an ass when I'm around her, then you're right."

"Why?" she asked.

"I have no idea. It just happens."

"Maybe because you like her and that worries you?" Laura replied, hitting the nail on the head.

I shrugged.

"She isn't Moira Finlay."

I snapped my head, meeting her gaze. It was filled with understanding.

"I know," I said roughly.

"She had an agenda, John. Quinn doesn't. She's working on making a life for herself and her daughter. Running a business." She looked reflective for a moment. "I like her. She is real and upfront. I think she was hurt too." She regarded me. "I think you two have more in common than you think."

"The only thing we have in common is that we strike sparks. We can barely hold a civil conversation."

"Maybe you need to try harder." She drained her beer. "Maybe a swing for her daughter is a good way to try."

"Is that why you came over here?"

She smiled. "I heard you ate at the Dill. Tammy says you even ordered dessert, something rare for you."

I groaned. "Is that what we're calling it now? The Dill?"

She laughed, not saying anything, but waiting for my explanation.

"I was hungry. Quinn's kid was there and told me to order the cake."

"I heard that too. You shared your lunch with her."

"She just showed up. I couldn't send her away."

She stood. "I also heard you and Quinn had an intense moment."

"Dammit. Someone saw? It was an accident. I didn't mean to kiss her."

Laura's eyebrows flew up. "*Kiss her?* I meant you saved her from falling, but that is way bigger news, brother. You kissed her?"

"It was by accident," I insisted.

She started to laugh. "Your lips jumped off your face onto hers?" She began walking away. "Oh boy, denial ain't just a river in Egypt, John. Make that swing and go see her. Man up."

She was still laughing as she climbed into her car. "Maybe you'll have another incident. Lord knows what might happen if your pants accidentally came off."

I glared as she backed up and drove down the driveway.

My pants were never coming off around Quinn.

Although the thought of that made my dick twitch.

Wasn't happening.

Saturday afternoon, I pulled up in front of Quinn's house. My hands felt clammy, and I wiped them on my jeans, watching as Quinn pushed a lawn mower across the front lawn. It was a fairly big yard, and I frowned, wondering if she was managing it okay.

I climbed from the truck, heading her way. She was busy, focused on her task, and she startled when I came into her view. She frowned as she shut off the lawn mower, wiping at her forehead.

"Mr. Elliott. Is there a problem?"

"John," I corrected. "And no, there isn't one."

She frowned. "You're here because…" She let her words trail off.

"I heard you wanted a swing for Abby on the oak tree."

"I thought she would like it. I can watch her from the porch. If you say it's okay."

"It's fine. I'm here to put it up."

She blinked. "I'm sorry?"

"I'm here to put up the swing."

"I haven't bought it yet."

I swallowed. "I made her one."

For a moment, there was shocked silence.

"You made her one," she repeated.

"Yes."

"You made a swing for my daughter."

"Yes."

"And you're here to put it up."

"Yes."

She looked around. "I feel as if I'm in an alternate universe."

I felt a grin pull on my lips.

"I wanted to make sure it was a good swing and hung properly." I paused. "So the tree wasn't damaged."

"So the tree wasn't damaged," she repeated. "That's why?"

"She's a good kid. I liked making her a swing."

A tender smile broke out on her face. "She is a good kid. And I thank you, John. Really."

I tried to ignore the way it felt when she said my name. I liked it far too much. "Is she around?"

"No, she was invited to a birthday party this afternoon. She was so excited. I was worried, you know? A new place, new people. I thought she'd be nervous, but she just waved me off and joined her new friends." She laughed self-consciously. "I had a hard time leaving her, but she was fine. I checked in twice, and Mandy's mom told me she was having a great time. I pick her up at four."

I saw the love for her child shining in her eyes. Heard it in the words as she expressed her worries. It helped unlock the small doubts I carried with me. Quinn was real. What you saw was what you got.

"Well then, let me get this installed, and she can have a surprise waiting for her."

"I can help," she offered tentatively.

"Great. Many hands, light work," I responded.

Her smile was unexpected. It was like a burst of sun after a storm. Bright, full, warm.

I wanted to bask in it. Make her smile for me again.

I was so fucked.

She held the ladder as I climbed up to the perfect branch.

"Will it hold her?" Quinn asked, a worried tone in her voice.

I swung myself onto the branch, swaying back and forth. "If it holds me, it'll hold Pumpkin."

She gasped. "John—careful. You might fall!"

Laughing, I dropped to the ground, standing in front of her. "See? Everything is fine."

She swatted my arm, and I winked at her. "That had the same effect as you kicking me. We need to work on your strength."

She blushed, the color on her cheeks doing something to me. My body tightened, and I had to fight not to react.

"I shouldn't have kicked you. I'm sorry."

Her words helped lighten the air around us again. "Not a problem. It was more as if a fly landed on my jeans than your foot."

She rolled her eyes. "I was having an off day."

I chuckled and stepped back. "Have another go then, darlin'."

She frowned. "That isn't fair. You're prepared. I need to get you when you least expect it. Catch you off guard so you fall like a dead tree."

I stared at her a moment, then began to laugh. Long, belly laughs that almost hurt. They hurt more than her foot could.

"Okay, Quinn." I wiped my eyes. "You prepare your secret attack."

She grinned, and we shared a light moment, our eyes meeting, her beautifully colored irises gleaming in the sun. She was stunning in her amusement. The sunlight caught highlights in her dark hair, casting a red and gold hue around her. She looked relaxed and comfortable. Happy. It was a good look on her.

"I'll try not to leave permanent damage."

I headed to the truck for the swing. "You do that."

We worked together seamlessly. I looped the ropes over the branch, securing them well, then added the swing, knotting the heavy rope tightly. "This would hold even me," I assured Quinn. "You can swing with her if you want. I made it large enough."

Quinn ran her hand over the smooth wood. "You painted it her favorite color."

"Of course."

She traced her finger over the decals I had added. The bright colors and big petals had caught my eye while I was picking up the paint, and I knew they were the perfect addition to the swing. Bob had side-eyed me while I was paying, but I'd refused to engage with him. I'd gotten out of the store as quickly as I could before he started to tease me.

"How did you do the flowers?"

"Oh, ah…" I trailed off, then cleared my throat. "I saw them at the hardware store and I thought Abby would like them. Jenny, the woman who ran the paint area, explained how to put them on, and then I sealed them under twenty layers of varnish. She won't get any splinters, and the flowers won't fade as much."

She knelt beside the swing, running her hand over the satin of the wood. "It's so amazing." She looked up, her eyes shining. "No one has ever done anything like this for her. Thank you."

I stared down, once again trying to lock my body down. I could see Quinn on her knees exactly the way she was now, but the scenario was totally changed. We were alone, in my bedroom, and neither of us was dressed. My cock jumped at the mental image, and I swore I almost felt her touch. Our eyes remained locked, and I felt the air around us change. Grow taut with tension. Her breathing picked up, and my heart began to gallop.

Then her phone rang, breaking the spell. She scrambled off her knees as I turned, bending to throw some tools back in the box.

"Hey, baby," she crooned, her voice sounding rougher than normal. She listened for a moment. "Are you sure? You really want to?" Again, she was quiet. "Okay. Let me speak to her mom."

I went to the truck, loading my tools back up. I returned as she hung up. "Everything okay?"

"Yes, they're having a barbecue and invited her to stay. I'll pick her up about seven now." She blinked, and I saw the glimmer of tears in her eyes. Concerned, I moved closer.

"Hey, you okay?"

She sniffed, wiping away the wetness. "Sorry, I'm being silly." She sighed. "I wanted her to find friends. To be a kid. Laugh, yell—" she pushed at the swing, making it move gently "—play outside."

"She didn't do those things before?"

"No." Quinn inhaled, letting it out slowly. "Her father didn't like noise. Dirt. Laughter. Color. Everything was black and white. We were expected to be quiet. Know our place." She looked down, scuffing her foot in the grass. "I couldn't do it anymore. I didn't want that for my daughter. I left him."

"That took courage," I said with honest admiration.

"I wish I had done it sooner."

"Sometimes you have to wait for the right time."

She sighed. "Well, I found it. I moved out, fought with him for months, then got my freedom. But he was still too close. My friend Cathy heard about the opportunity here and called me." She smiled, looking around. "I found this place. We got a fresh start."

"Are you concerned he'll come looking for you?"

Her laugh was bitter. "No. He's getting remarried. He was happy his past mistakes weren't going to be around to embarrass him anymore."

"You're not a mistake. Neither is Pumpkin," I insisted, almost growling the words.

"He thought so."

"Obviously, he is an asshole."

She began to laugh. "Yes, yes, he is."

"And so am I. I apologize."

She shook her head. "There's a difference. He wanted to hurt me. Control me. You just…didn't like me."

I blew out a long breath. "You're wrong, Quinn. The problem was I did like you. I still do. I was just reacting to my own screwed-up past, and I took it out on you."

"I guess we both need to move forward."

I stuck out my hand. "We do. I'm John."

She let me take her hand, my large palm engulfing hers. "Quinn."

For a second, neither of us spoke. Then she smiled. "Can I offer you a drink, John? To say thanks for the swing?"

"I'd like that."

I followed her to the porch, and she held open the door. Inside, I looked around, noticing the hominess of the small space. The toys in the corner. The blankets and cushions on the sofa.

"Check out her room if you want," Quinn called.

It was easy to identify which one was Abby's. The bright-pink walls, the frilly curtains and bedspread. The toys strewn around. I had to admit the color was too much for me, but I knew the kid loved it, and that was all that mattered.

Unable to help myself, I peeked into Quinn's room. The walls were a soft green, her bed some sort of wicker. It was light and feminine, and it smelled like her as I inhaled the fragrance that lingered in the air.

I hurried back down the hall, not wanting to be caught snooping. She came from the kitchen with a tray, and I opened the door, sitting beside her on the porch. She handed me a drink and picked up a plate. "You must be hungry."

I eyed the snacks with appreciation, taking a sausage roll and biting down. The flaky pastry and spicy meat made me groan.

"These are incredible."

"I was thinking of adding them to the menu. On an appetizer plate."

I nodded, taking another bite. "I'd order them," I muttered around a mouthful.

"Hell getting cold again?" she teased.

"Positively frigid."

"Good. But don't let Abby talk you into sharing your food."

I chuckled. "I didn't mind. Cody does the same."

"Your nephew, right?"

"Yep."

"He was showing off his new bike at the park. Said his uncle J bought it for him as a birthday gift." She studied me. "Told me his uncle J is the best guy around."

"He exaggerates."

She picked up her drink, taking a sip. "Somehow I think he doesn't. I'm beginning to see past your big, bad bear routine, John."

I picked up my drink, not saying anything.

Yet, somehow, the news made me smile.

8

JOHN

I got up to leave, thanking Quinn for the snack. She frowned.

"What?"

"After all your hard work, you should see her reaction when she sees her swing. She'll be so excited."

"Nah, it's fine. I need to get home to the chickens and cows."

She stood. "Thank you."

I nodded. "Yep."

She put her hand on my arm and rolled up on her toes. I knew she was going to kiss my cheek again, and once more, I found myself turning my head so our lips met. Except this time, no one was around. No one to break the bubble that suddenly surrounded us.

I wrapped an arm around her waist, pulling her closer. She slid her hand up my arm, her fingers grasping my neck. I groaned as I flicked my tongue on her lips, and she opened for me.

I kissed her more. Deeper. She kissed me back. I held her tighter, and she whimpered softly. Our mouths separated, then came back together, unable to stay apart. I kissed her until I couldn't breathe. Until her grip was so tight I knew I was holding her up. Then I pulled away, letting her lay her head on my chest. My breathing was fast, my chest pumping needed oxygen into my bloodstream. She was quiet, her body melding to mine perfectly.

I eased back, meeting her eyes. I saw no regret, no censure in them. I touched her cheek.

"Thank you, darlin'."

She smiled and turned her head, kissing my palm. The alarm on her phone went off, and I bent, handing it to her. "Go get Abby. I hope she likes her swing."

She took her phone, clutching it in her hand. "She will."

"Good."

I walked away, but this time, it wasn't out of anger. I knew if I stayed, I would drag her into the house and kiss her until we were both desperate. Then I would have her. I wouldn't stop until she was screaming my name with my cock buried deep inside her.

And she had a daughter waiting.

I slid into my truck, already missing the taste and feel of her.

Then I drove home.

Alone and lonelier than I could recall feeling in a long time.

Quinn was on my mind all night. The sensation of peace and tranquility I had simply sitting with her. Enjoying her company. The way her laughter made me smile. She was witty and charming.

And the way I felt when I kissed her was unexpected and disarming.

She fit against me well, her body molding to mine. The taste of her lingered for hours, the fragrance of her on my skin. I wanted more of it. She was the last thing on my mind when I fell asleep and the first thought I had when I woke up—aching and hard for her.

It was her name I groaned out in the shower as I took

myself in hand, desperate for relief. The orgasm took the edge off, but I wanted more.

I wanted her.

I sighed as I poured a coffee, heading outside. I had been up for hours, checking the crops and the animals. I had a basket of eggs to go to town, which I planned on doing later, unless Cody happened to show up looking for more cash for his bank account. He was fascinated by the column of numbers in the passbook he had. He loved watching them grow, and I had to laugh at the fact that he was making lots of small deposits so he could see the total change all the time. He had decided on a new sled for the winter and was running recon on ideas for Christmas for his mom and dad. He'd dropped a few questions my way, and I played along, pretending to be none the wiser. He hadn't figured out yet that by telling me about the sled, he had just solved my dilemma for what to get him. His money could stay in the bank.

I sat on the rocker, mentally going over a list of what I had to do later. Luckily, it was Sunday, and I tried to keep things to a minimum. I had a few chores— laundry and inside tasks. The farm was taken care of, aside from feeding the animals again later. It would be a quiet day, something I normally enjoyed. But somehow, today, it felt solitary. I knew I could drive to Laura's and spend the afternoon there, but the truth was, it wasn't what I wanted to do, and Laura wasn't the woman I wanted to see.

I had just shaken my head at the strange thoughts when I heard a car, and I glanced up, expecting my sister. But it wasn't her vehicle pulling up to the house. It was an SUV I recognized. When Quinn stepped out, stopping to help Abby from the back seat and pulling a huge hamper from the trunk, I felt the stirrings of something in my chest. Pleasure. Happiness.

I stood, a smile pulling at my mouth. I walked to the edge of the porch. "Hey."

"Hi," Quinn said with a smile, while Abby grinned at me, jumping foot to foot.

"Hey, Pumpkin. You got ants in your pants?"

She laughed, the high-pitched sound making me chuckle with her.

"No, Farmer John! I'm excited!"

I stepped off the porch. "About?"

She flung herself at me, wrapping her arms around my waist. "My swing! I love it!"

"I'm glad." I bent and lifted her, hoisting her to my chest. "Have you tried it?"

Quinn made an amused sound. "Tried it? I could

barely get her off it last night, and she was up and on it this morning before six."

"I love it! I can go high, and the seat is big enough that Enid and Fluffy can swing with me. Except—" she looked me in the eye, serious "—they keep falling off. Can you make them a seat belt, Farmer John?"

Quinn shook her head, and I smirked. "I can do that."

"Yay—I told you he could, Momma. He can do anything."

I met Quinn's gaze. It was gentle and warm this morning. Our eyes locked and held, that warmth in her expression flowing between us.

"What's in the basket?" I asked.

"Momma and me made a picnic."

"A picnic?"

Abby nodded enthusiastically. "To say thank you."

"It's for you," Quinn explained. "For lunch or dinner —whatever you want."

"Fried chicken," Abby added. "And *tato* salad."

"Any pickles?" I asked with a wink.

"Lots," Abby assured me.

"And you ladies will stay, of course."

"As long as we're not interrupting. Otherwise, we'll leave it for you whenever you want it."

Abby rolled her eyes. "He asked us, Momma. You said you hoped he would."

Quinn's cheeks reddened, and once again, the sight of her blush brought forth a rush of desire and protectiveness. It was disconcerting, yet somehow, I didn't mind it.

"It's settled, then," I stated firmly. "We're having a picnic. And I know the perfect spot."

Abby threw up her arms. "Yay!"

Quinn and I shared an amused look, not saying anything, but inside, I was throwing up my arms too and celebrating.

Suddenly, the day didn't seem as desolate.

Quinn looked around, entranced. "It's so pretty here!"

I had to agree with her. "Laura and I loved it here as kids." I chuckled. "My parents loved that we loved it. Close enough for us to be safe, but far enough away to give them some downtime."

"Your parents lived nearby?"

"Just down the road a little closer to town. I cut through the fields so often, I wore down a trail."

"Is the house still there?"

"No, we sold it after they passed, and the new owners tore it down and built a new place." I shrugged. "I loved the farmhouse and Laura wanted her own place without the memories. It was best to sell it. But this spot is filled with memories for us."

I watched her excitement, feeling the stirrings of pride. The little creek was just behind the house to the left, bordered by trees and grasses. My dad and gramps had brooked up a small area that gave us a place to swim. It was about four feet deep at the shallow end, dipping into eight by the other side, and twelve feet around, and it was heaven on a hot day. The water flowed over the edge, making a small waterfall that was fun too. I had added some decking beside it a few years ago and put in a firepit. There was an old table and chairs that had seen better days, but they worked. Cody loved coming here, and the spot was well used. Swimming, barbecues, fires complete with marshmallows.

And today, the company of the cute kid and her mother, who was somehow proving to be irresistible.

Quinn unpacked the food, and my mouth watered at the fried chicken, potato salad, and the brownies she put out. The container of pickles made me chuckle, but I knew they'd be tasty.

I bit into the chicken, suddenly famished. "Wow. That is incredible." I took another bite, savoring the flavor. "Best fried chicken I've ever had."

"We have it at the Dill on Wednesdays."

"I'll make a note of that."

"Your other place of residence cooling off?" Quinn asked with a grin as she took a bite of her chicken.

"Permanent iceberg."

She looked pleased. "Ah."

"Farmer John?" Abby asked.

"Yeah?"

"Can I swim after lunch?"

"Sure. If it's okay with your mom."

Quinn ruffled Abby's hair. "Good thing I have your suit in the back."

"Will you swim, Momma?"

"I don't have a suit."

"You're wearing a T-shirt," I pointed out. Grinning, I leaned close. "You got underwear on under those overalls, darlin', or are you commando?"

She pursed her lips, trying to look affronted but failing. "Of course I do."

"Probably covers you more than a bikini. I can give you another shirt to wear after."

"Are you sure?"

The thought of her wearing my clothes did something to me. It made me want to beat my chest and roar out in victory. I glanced up at the sun, wondering if I was suffering from heatstroke.

Roar out in victory?

But her grin made it all better. "Okay, then."

Game on.

Abby swam like a little fish, splashing and going underwater as if she'd been doing it all her life. Quinn watched her from the side, her wet T-shirt glued to her skin. I tried not to notice the shadow of her taut nipples under the thin material when she would stand to watch Abby. Unfortunately, my cock did, and I was grateful for the coolness of the water and the fact that it hid my arousal. She had long legs, and the image of them wrapped around me as I drove into her kept filtering through my brain, even as I tried to stop it. I didn't understand how, in such a short time, I had gone from disliking Quinn to wanting to be close to her. To get to know her.

Internally, I shook my head. I had been attracted to her the first night at the fair. Even during our tumultuous meetings, I found her appealing. I had been too much of a jerk to admit exactly how tempting.

Abby called for us to watch as she dove under the water, splashing us as she kicked. I laughed as I wiped my face. "She loves the water," I observed.

"Yes. I put her in swimming lessons when she was a baby. She has always loved it. We spent a lot of time at the public pool."

"My dad taught me to swim. My mom wasn't a huge fan of water."

"My ex wasn't a fan of anything," she murmured. "Especially us."

"Sounds like an idiot."

She sighed. "I was the idiot for staying and hoping."

I glanced at her. She was staring at Abby, her shoulders hunched as if in pain.

"Maybe you were the one with the heart," I said gently. "The brave one."

She shrugged, but I noticed her shoulders straightened a little.

"Anyway, she loves to swim, and she loves a bath. Hates the rain."

"Really?"

"Storms bother her. The wind and thunder."

"We get some bad ones here."

"I already made a place in my closet. We hide together. I'm not a big fan either, so we camp out. I read to her, and we use a portable light and a radio for music. I try to make it fun. Distract her. The worst is when the power goes out and everything is dark and the lantern runs out of power and I've forgotten to buy more batteries."

"What do you do then?"

"Sing to her."

"Who sings to you?"

She turned her head and met my eyes. "No one. I have to be strong for her."

In that moment, I realized how close we were sitting. Our thighs were pressed together, our shoulders touching. All it would take was the tilt of my head, and I could kiss her. The draw was strong, her closeness weaving a spell around us. I began to lower my head when I heard my sister's voice behind us.

"John!"

I backed away from Quinn, creating some distance. Laura, Bob, and Cody appeared, towels in hand. "I figured I'd find you here. It's hot and we——" Laura stopped midsentence. "Oh, you have company." Her eyes grew wide when she realized who it was.

"Come join us," I invited her.

Cody rushed forward, but Laura stood where she was. "Are we interrupting?"

"No," I said easily, not wanting to upset Quinn. "We had a picnic, and we're cooling off. Lots of room."

"Hi, Laura," Quinn greeted her.

"Hi, yourself. You know Bob."

He waved, shucking off his shirt and following Cody into the swimming hole. Cody was chatting with Abby, no shyness between the two kids. Laura eyed me, then set down her bags, coming over to the spot we were sitting. Abby called to her mom, who went over to see what she wanted, and Laura slid into the water, giving me the once-over.

"You don't usually have tenants over for a swim," she muttered under her breath.

"She brought me lunch to say thanks for the swing I built and installed. It was hot. It seemed like the right thing to do."

I was silent. "Besides, she's not a usual tenant."

"Farmer John! Come watch me do some handstands," Abby called.

I stood, and my sister grabbed my hand. "We are going to talk later."

There was no point in refusing. Laura would be relentless until she got what she wanted.

"Later."

9

JOHN

We ended up grilling hot dogs, and with the leftover fried chicken and the tossed salad Laura had brought with her, we convinced Quinn and Abby to stay for supper. After, the kids sat on the steps, eating huge slices of ice-cold watermelon. The grown-ups ate theirs in a bowl. Far less messy but, judging from the laughter from a few feet away, far less enjoyable.

"You settling in all right?" Laura asked.

"Oh yes," Quinn said. "She loves her school. The staff I hired, especially Tammy, have made it so easy. She takes the morning shift, I come in after taking Abby to school, and I get to pick her up. Our hours work well. If I have to stay late, Mrs. Grainger takes her, and I pick her up there." Quinn shook her head. "A bit of a dream, how quickly our life has found a rhythm, to be honest."

"What will you do for the summer?"

"I have her in a few camps. Swimming, a kids cooking camp, and a music one at the school. I'll hire extra staff to cover the days I need to be at home. She can come to the restaurant if needed. Mrs. Grainger will take her at times too."

"I can help out."

Everyone stopped and looked at me, and I shrugged. "Pumpkin and I get on well. I've looked after Cody."

Laura smiled. "I can help too if needed. And there is a great camp Cody goes to every summer—but it's a stay for a week place. Would she like that?"

Quinn was quiet for a moment. "I'm not sure. Since the incid—" she stopped talking, clearing her throat "—I mean the divorce, she is clingy, but I could ask her."

I shared a look with my sister. Quinn had stumbled over the word incident. Not divorce.

What had that fucker done?

I hadn't even realized I had curled my hands into fists or made a noise until Laura leaned over, patting my arm. "Take a breath, big brother. Maybe two. This isn't the time."

Quinn regarded me with wide eyes, and I forced

myself to relax. She blinked and turned to look at Abby, and I exhaled a long gust of air.

What the hell was wrong with me today?

"I can go with you if you want to check it out," Laura volunteered. "Cody's been going since he was six. He loves it. I know the owners well, and then you can decide if you want to broach the subject with her."

"Sounds good," Quinn replied.

The conversation turned to other things. Crops, the restaurant, the troublesome woman Laura was dealing with. Bob shared some funny stories from the store, and before it grew dark, the kids ran around kicking the soccer ball and climbing the fence to see the cows.

When they came back, Abby stood beside my chair and yawned. Loudly. I bit back my amusement and patted my knee. She climbed up, snuggling in as if she did it every day. I put my arm around her, still talking to Bob about the apartment units' plans. I met Quinn's shocked gaze, and I stopped.

"Sorry. Did I overstep?"

"No," she replied. "I've never seen her do that."

"I like Farmer John," Abby muttered sleepily. "He's big, and his hug is nice."

"There you have it," Laura stated. "Good hugs."

Cody laughed. "Uncle J gives the best." Then he grinned sheepishly. "Next to you and Dad, of course."

Laura ruffled his hair. "It's okay, kiddo. Uncle J has always given the best hugs."

We talked as darkness descended. Cody read a book he had brought, sitting close to the lamps on the table.

Quinn leaned in. "We should go. She's asleep, and if I get home fast enough, she'll stay that way."

I looked down in amusement. Abby was snuggled in, and I had been stroking her hair, not even realizing it. One of her little hands gripped my shirt, and the other was tucked under her chin. "I'll carry her to the car."

I followed her as Laura, Bob, and Cody said goodnight and headed inside.

I slid Abby into her booster seat, snapping on the seat belt. I shut the door quietly so as not to wake her, and I went to the driver's side.

"I still have your shirt," Quinn whispered.

I had loved knowing under her overalls it was my shirt she wore, the sleeves too big and the shoulders hanging down her arms. "Keep it."

She tilted her head up, smiling. "I'll wash it and bring it back."

"No rush."

"Thank you for today. It was wonderful."

"Thanks for the company and the fried chicken. My family ate my lunches for the week."

"I'll bring you more."

I reached over and ran my finger down her cheek. "I'd like that."

"Do you know what I'd like?"

"Tell me," I replied, my voice dropping to a husky whisper.

"I heard your hugs are the best. I'd like to find out."

I pulled her close, holding her in my embrace. She fit against me, looping her arms around my waist. I held her tight, breathing her in. Then I slipped my fingers under her chin and stared down at her. "Do you want to know what I want?"

"I'm hoping it's the same thing I want," she murmured, kissing my thumb that lingered near her mouth.

With a groan, I captured her lips with mine and kissed her. There was nothing gentle and sweet about it. It was hard and deep. Claiming. I explored her, drinking her in, sliding my hand to her ass and cupping it. She responded, her breathy sounds egging me on. My cock hardened, trapped between us, and it was only the sleeping child in the back seat that stopped me from pinning Quinn against the vehicle and ravishing her completely.

I heard the squeak of the wooden door, and regretfully, I eased back, but not before dropping three fast kisses to Quinn's wet lips. She blinked up at me, her gaze unfocused and filled with passion.

"Call me when you get home."

"I don't have your number."

I took her phone and programmed myself in, then called so I had her number.

"Call me."

She climbed in, starting the car. She shifted into drive and looked at me, rolling down her window.

"What is it?" I asked.

"They were right. Best hugs ever."

Then with a wink and a wave, she drove off.

I waited until her taillights disappeared and went inside to face the inquisition.

10

QUINN

bby stayed asleep during the drive home, not waking even as I slipped her into bed. I wasn't worried about a bath—she'd been swimming enough all day. I left her T-shirt on and tucked her in, making sure Enid was beside her. I looked around for Fluffy, but the bear wasn't there. I must have left her in the back seat. I would go and get her before I went to bed, or Abby would be upset in the morning if she couldn't find her.

I left the night-light on as usual and headed to my room. I took off my overalls, hesitating before I pulled off the shirt John had given me to wear. I clutched the collar, bringing the soft white fabric to my nose and inhaling deeply. He smelled so good every time I was close. It reminded me of summer rain and fresh-cut grass. And since I was wearing an article of his clothing, it was stronger, more saturated, and I had to admit, I loved it.

I left it on the bed and took a shower, washing my hair, and I put on a pair of loose shorts. Unable to resist, I slid his shirt back on, once again surrounded by his scent. I headed to the kitchen after peeking in on Abby, poured a cold glass of water, and settled on the sofa with my Kindle. Except I kept staring at the page, not seeing the words, but recalling the day. The past two days.

Thinking especially about John.

His unexpected visit yesterday and the swing he'd made Abby. How easy it had been with him, helping, watching him as he put it up, his first priority her safety. He had no idea how incredibly sexy he was swinging himself up on the branch to test it out. Climbing the ladder and knotting the ropes. Even the care that went into his creation of the simple swing itself. The bright pink he had painted it. The decorative flowers and the many layers of varnish to seal it so she wouldn't get a sliver.

All for a little girl he barely knew.

It was more than her father had done her entire life.

Images of the last hours flitted through my mind. John looking pleased and excited with the picnic lunch. His smile was almost shy as he showed us his house. The huge central kitchen, with a good-sized dining room and a living area. There were four bedrooms, two on either side of the kitchen, plus an office and a large storeroom. The furniture was older, comfortable, and the entire house had a loved and used look. The well-worn floors gleamed in the light, glossy with age. There was nothing pretentious or fancy about it. He was excited to take us to the swimming hole. His honest and lavish praise for the lunch I had made brought a smile to my mouth and color to my cheeks. He seemed to like that.

I liked the way his chest rippled as he pulled off his shirt to get into the water. His torso was tight and ripped. His arms strong, his biceps flexing as he moved. His legs were powerful, his thighs thick, the muscles bunching in sexy waves under the skin. I'd had to look away, the lust that flared inside me simply by looking at him almost bringing me to my knees. I had never felt anything like it.

And when he'd finally kissed me again, I almost exploded. His lips were surprisingly soft, considering the cross words he often uttered. But when he was kissing me, he was completely sweet. And sexy. He made some low, growly sounds in his throat. His chest rumbled against mine in pleasure. His embrace was tight, his caresses indulgent. He made me forget about everything, but him. Us. The sensations he brought out. My past didn't matter. Our heated interactions faded away. There was only him and me.

I sighed, running a finger over my lips. I swore I could still feel the possession of his mouth on mine. And I liked it. Maybe too much.

I hadn't expected this. Planned for it. I planned for everything.

Farmer John wasn't on my bingo card.

And yet, there he was. The big free space in the middle.

A soft knock startled me, and I frowned as I stood. I wasn't expecting anyone. A small tremor went through me, but I shook my head. Preston made it perfectly clear he didn't care where we went or what I did, as long as it didn't involve him. His exact words were "the farther away, the better." Those had been the last words he'd spoken as he signed away his parental rights and the divorce papers. Then he walked away, not bothering to look back.

The knock came again, and I approached the door. "Hello?" I called out.

"Hey, it's me," John replied.

I opened the door, meeting his warm gaze. It was so different from the frosty one I had gotten used to seeing that, for a moment, all I could do was stare. He grinned at me. "Cat got your tongue, darlin'?"

I shook my head and stepped back, indicating for him to come inside. I shut the door and turned to face him. "Everything okay? I texted you that we got home."

"Oh yeah, everything is fine," he assured me. "I got the text." He winked. "I liked the little x at the end, by the way."

I had hesitated about adding that, but in the end, I had. Now I was glad.

"I had meant to give you some fresh eggs and forgot." He handed me a small basket.

"You didn't have to drive all the way over here."

"It wasn't a problem."

Then he held up Fluffy. "But given Pumpkin's love for her bear, I was afraid not having this when she woke up might be."

"Oh, I thought it was in the SUV!"

"I found this on the ground after you left," he explained. "I hated the thought of her upset. I know Cody used to freak out if he couldn't find his blanket." He chuckled, his eyes dancing. "He still has it in his room. He says it's no big deal, but I know he keeps it close."

"You came over with it so she wouldn't be upset," I whispered, my throat tight.

"And so you had fresh eggs for breakfast. A good start for both of you."

Some men would have called. Others wouldn't have bothered. Most wouldn't have noticed it lying there until the next day—if then. But he did. And he brought it over, along with some fresh eggs so our morning would be better.

This man.

This man who liked to grump and let people think he was unapproachable.

He was anything but.

I launched myself at him, my mouth on his before I could think. He immediately wrapped me in his arms, kissing me back with utter abandonment. Fluffy fell to the floor, unheeded. In seconds, John had turned, pressing me against the wall beside the doorway he'd walked in through. His body was hard, massive, like sculpted marble, pressing into my softer body, our forms melded together. I wrapped my legs around his hips, and he cupped my nape, keeping me close to his mouth. I moaned as he slid his hand along my bare skin, his fingers inching upward on my thighs. I gasped in his mouth as his fingers grazed the edge of my underwear, some small piece of my brain screaming it was too soon and he needed to stop. I wasn't listening to that voice right now. The glide of his tongue along mine was erasing every other thought from my head.

Then his phone rang, breaking the moment. He stilled, pulling back his head, meeting my eyes.

"I can ignore that."

"But you probably shouldn't," I whispered regretfully.

He nodded, dropping another fast kiss to my mouth, then set me on my feet. But he didn't move away, answering his phone with a quiet hello. He listened for a moment. "They *what*?" He shook his head with a frustrated groan. "Okay. Tell them I'll be there right away."

He slipped his phone into his pocket, hanging his head. "That was Laura. One of my tenants just tried to hang a picture and somehow drilled into a wire. They have no power now."

"Oh dear."

He stepped back, and I missed his warmth right away. "I have to go look and call Fred, the local electrician. He's not gonna be happy." He ran his thumb over my bottom lip. "He can join the club."

"Probably best, though," I whispered, my voice raspy-sounding.

"I can't say I entirely agree, but perhaps."

He bent and kissed me again, his hand once more going to my nape and cupping my head. "I could just make them wait a bit."

I laughed, knowing he didn't mean it. "Go do your landlord duties."

"If you want to pull a couple wires later…" He trailed off with a wink.

He made me laugh, and I was glad when he joined in.

"Okay, I'll go." He stood straight with a sigh, opening the door. "But we're not finished, Quinn. Not by a long shot."

Then he was gone.

I didn't hear from him that night or the next day. Part of me was disappointed, although I had no claims on him or his time. I knew he was a busy man with his farm, his leases, and whatever else he did. Which, around here, seemed to be a lot. I heard his name often, dropped into conversations at the restaurant.

"We should ask John about that."

"John helped on that house. He'd know."

"I can already taste John's corn. I can hardly wait until harvest time."

"You heard about his plans for the old school? He's always thinking ahead. It'll be good for the town. Maybe bring in another new business. I sure like this one."

That remark made me smile. The restaurant was doing well. My divorce money had come in, as well as Preston's guilt money for deserting Abby. At least, that was what I called it. His lawyer termed it a lump sum payment in lieu of child support. Either way, we would have no contact anymore. He wanted no information, pictures, or chances to visit or know his daughter. He even hinted she might not be his and I should be grateful for his generosity. It took every ounce of strength I had not to retaliate. My lawyer had kept me calm, and I'd simply shaken my head. *"Get a DNA test, then," I murmured. "She has your color eyes."*

He had shaken his head. "I just want this over."

Of course he did. That was why it finally happened. He'd met someone new, someone more worthy of his social standing and lifestyle. He wanted to be free, and he was willing to pay handsomely for me to go away.

I was willing to take the money and no longer be subjected to him.

And now, I could buy the building and truly call it my own. I would stay in the small house I was renting for now. We liked it, and it was all we needed.

I came out of the kitchen toward the end of the day, smiling and filling a few coffee cups, and carrying the tray to clear the last couple of tables. The bell rang, and I forced myself to smile as I looked up, hoping it would be a takeout order or someone looking for something simple. It had been a busy day, and I wanted to go get Abby and head home.

John stood in the doorway, his massive shoulders almost blocking the light. He hesitated, looking around, then he met my gaze, and a smile broke out on his face.

My God, he was handsome when he smiled. His lips curled, revealing straight white teeth. His eyes crinkled, the blue of his irises still visible in his tanned face. His dimples appeared, and he had laugh lines that made him even more attractive somehow.

He shut the door, coming closer. "I know it's late, Quinn. I was wondering about getting a sandwich?"

Up close, I could see he was tired. Weariness was etched on his skin, and his eyes were dimmer than usual.

"Of course. We're still open for another forty-five minutes. Anything you want."

"Coffee would be great. And whatever you have left."

"Sit down," I instructed. "I'll bring you something," I offered, wondering why my voice was so husky-sounding.

He lifted his eyebrows, his gaze focused on my mouth. "Great. Anything you give me, I'll take."

I had to fan myself in the kitchen after I set down a cup of coffee for him. Clint, the cook, looked up. "I heard John's voice. What do you need?"

"What do we have left?"

"Soup. Sandwich fixings. Anything frozen. I haven't turned off the fryers."

"No, he needs something solid. Do a big bowl of soup and a grilled bacon and cheese sandwich. Triple-decker with tomatoes."

"Done."

I grabbed the last salad and a large glass of ice water. I had noticed John liked his beverages cold. I added ranch to his salad, already knowing that was his favorite dressing, and went out front. Chloe was cleaning off the last of the tables, and aside from John, there was a table of four older men who came in most days for pie and coffee.

I carried his salad and water to the table, sliding it in front of him. "Start with this. The rest will be out in a couple of minutes."

"Great." He cleared his throat. "Can you sit?"

"In a few moments. Eat," I urged.

He picked up his fork and dug in, crunching the lettuce and cucumbers. "Delish," he hummed.

I helped Chloe with a couple of things, then headed to the back, picking up the huge plate. The bowl was massive, and I chuckled. "Is that one of our serving dishes?"

Clint grinned. "John is known for his big appetite."

I carried it to John's table, sliding it in front of him. His eyes widened at the sight of the meal.

"You joining me?"

"Not to eat."

"You think I can eat all this?"

I fixed him with a look, and he grinned. "I see my reputation preceded me."

"It did. Eat. You look like you could fall down."

He dipped his spoon in the bowl, groaning. "I love beef barley soup."

"I make it myself."

"Even better."

He ate steadily, his manners impeccable. He hummed and praised the food, and I let him eat, pleased to see the color coming back to his face and the light glint in his eyes again.

Chloe cashed out the last table and waved to them as they left. I called out my thanks, then told Chloe to lock up. I grabbed a cup of coffee and slid into the booth across from John.

"I think I'm going to change the hours to three," I mused. "We rarely get anyone after two-thirty."

John nodded. "More time with Abby."

"Yep. I can start on the next day prep and get home sooner."

"Good plan, then."

"Why do you look so tired, John?"

He chewed and swallowed a bite of his sandwich, wiping his mouth. "The wire the tenant hit was major. It caused a small fire, which we had to clean up and get checked to make sure there wasn't more hidden in the walls, then I had to have a bunch of rewiring done. One of my neighbor's donkeys went rogue and busted down a fence I had to fix before they trampled my crops. Laura's odd client went crazy and accused her of holding back the perfect house for her. She rampaged her office, and Laura called me, terrified, and Bob and I rushed down and had to call the cops on this woman. Turns out the house she thought Laura was hiding was an ad in the paper she'd seen for a model home in another province that used a small-town background from here. Laura has convinced her to look elsewhere for a house." He scrubbed his face. "It's been a hell of a couple of days."

"Is she okay?"

"Yeah, she's fine. The woman has moved on. Last Laura heard, she was booking a flight to Ohio. Laura didn't press charges, but the woman's husband is paying for all the damages."

"Wow."

He reached across the table, taking my hand. "All of that kept me from you, Quinn. I was so exhausted when I got home last night at two a.m., I fell asleep facedown at the kitchen table while eating a bowl of cereal."

"Good thing you didn't drown in the milk."

That made him laugh. "I was up at five working the fields, then back to the house to finish up the interior repairs."

"Do you pay for that?"

He took another bite, chewing and looking thoughtful. "I shouldn't. They caused the damage. But I'm helping pay. She was trying to hang their first family picture and somehow missed the stud and went right into the wire running up the side of it. Fred gave me a break on the work, and they will repaint. I'm glad they didn't burn down the house. They're a nice young couple. He works in the city hall office."

"You're a good man."

He rolled his eyes. "What good would it do me if I saddled them with a huge bill so they couldn't pay their rent? I guarantee she'll be more careful next time. In fact, she'll call me. Or wait for her husband to get home. Fred advised her to look and see if there was an outlet box on the stud before hammering in a nail next time. I think she learned her lesson."

"I was worried when you didn't call," I confessed. "But I'm glad to see you here."

He was silent for a moment, finishing his sandwich. "I'm sorry I worried you. I was so busy putting out fires, but I should have texted at least." He paused and looked dismayed. "Aside from my sister, I'm not used to having someone to worry about me. I'm not used to checking in."

"I understand."

"I'll do better."

He emptied his soup bowl and sat back. "Incredible," he muttered.

I got the coffeepot and filled our cups, then slid the last piece of blueberry pie in front of him. Chloe came out from the kitchen, waving goodbye. I locked the door behind her. Clint called out goodnight, leaving from the back.

"They're gone already?"

"Yep. I guarantee the kitchen is spotless. Chloe has the tables set for morning. Normally, I make the pie crusts for tomorrow or bake a cake. Put on the roast to cook overnight. Then I head home."

"You work hard."

"You do as well."

He sliced off a hunk of pie, chewing it. "God, woman, you can cook. I'm so glad hell froze over."

I laughed, resting my chin on my hand. "John—may I ask something?"

Instantly, I had his attention. He sat straighter, focused on me. I loved his intensity. "Anything, darlin'."

"Can I ask what we're doing?"

"I assume you mean in a broader spectrum than having coffee right now."

"Yes."

"I don't know," he admitted. "I was attracted to you from the start. Then we argued, and things went downhill. We seemed to strike sparks every time we were in the vicinity of each other." He regarded me for a moment. "We still do but in an entirely different way."

"So, you're still attracted to me."

He chuckled. "Quinn, even when you were driving me mad, I was attracted to you. That never stopped."

"So, what are we?" I asked.

He smiled. It was his gentle smile—the one that softened his eyes and made him look younger. The frown lines on his forehead disappeared, and he looked almost vulnerable.

"What are we?" he asked. "Again, I would admit to being unsure, but I do know this. We're something, and we're important. I think how important is up to you. You lead, Quinn. I'm ready to follow."

11

JOHN

Q uinn blinked at me, letting my words soak in.

"That's quite the statement, Mr. Elliott."

"I'm aware. And I meant it."

She swallowed, looking past my shoulder. "I like you, John. And I felt, *feel*, the same way. Even when we were disagreeing, I was attracted to you." She sighed, pushing back a stray lock of hair from her forehead. I tried not to smile as it fell back and she brushed it away again. I leaned forward, tucking it behind her ear.

"But?" I asked, keeping my voice level.

"I wondered if one of the reasons I liked disagreeing with you was because I felt safe enough to do so. Somehow I sensed there was a line, and you would never cross it."

I frowned. "Your ex?"

"He wasn't the nice man I thought him to be when I married him."

"Tell me."

She looked around. "Here?"

"We're alone. The door is locked. We can go into the kitchen, and you can do your prep while you talk if that would help." I sensed this would be a huge leap of faith for her to tell me and she would be nervous. Keeping her hands busy might be a good idea.

She thought about it, then nodded. "Yes. I'll make my pie crusts."

I followed her to the kitchen, staying out of the way as she gathered her supplies. I let her lead, giving her the time she needed to gather her thoughts.

"I met Preston Dutton at a friend's party. He seemed nice. Polite. Handsome. Good manners. We had a great conversation, and he asked for my number."

"I thought your last name was Harper."

She nodded. "I changed it back when we divorced. I didn't want any connection to him. I legally changed Abby's name as well."

I nodded in understanding. "How old were you when you met him?"

"Too young. Eighteen. He was older. I was taking business courses, and he was just graduating from finance. I told him my dream of having a little diner someday. Living in a pretty house and having kids. He told me he wanted to give me a big house and a big family. We became inseparable. I thought he was perfect. We wanted the same things. We had the same goals."

"Did your parents like him?" I asked as she measured and mixed.

"I lost my parents when I was eight. Until then, life was pretty normal. By then, my grandparents were older and in a home. I had to go into foster care." She looked at me, the pain in her eyes evident. "I never had a home or a family after that."

"So that's why it was so important to you," I said, understanding.

"Yes. His parents, on the other hand, didn't really like me, but he didn't care. We eloped less than a year after we met. He graduated, we moved, he got a job and rose up the company ladder fast. He worked constantly."

"Not easy on a relationship."

"No." She paused as she separated the dough into balls, wrapping it and putting it in the fridge. She leaned against the counter. "I worked in a small restaurant, learning the ropes. I loved it. He, on the other hand, hated it. Made me quit and told me it was beneath me. He couldn't have a wife who 'slung hash' for a living."

"Nothing wrong with honest work."

"That was what I believed. I thought he did too. The boy I married disappeared. And he became a man I didn't recognize." She gazed around the kitchen for a moment, sadness etched on her face. "He changed. Everything he said he loved about me was now tedious and beneath him. I was an embarrassment most of the time."

"You could never be an embarrassment."

"To him, I was. I got my house, all right. One he picked. Huge, ostentatious. Cold. He had it decorated and refused to let me touch it. I had to drive an expensive car. Dress a certain way. I wasn't allowed to even think about my dreams anymore. Everything was about him and his career. I got pregnant because he decided it was good for his image." She sighed, rubbing her hand over her eyes. "That wasn't what he told me, of course, but it slipped later. He got me drunk, and we had sex without a condom. I was shocked to find out I was pregnant. He was smug. Later, I found out why, and I was furious. Not," she explained quickly, "that I was pregnant. I was thrilled. But the way he did it."

"I can understand that."

"We grew apart—especially him. Other than for his image, he wanted nothing to do with Abby. And little to do with me. I was trapped in a marriage with someone whose favorite thing to do was tell me all the ways I disappointed him."

"Bastard."

"Yes. And as I found out, he simply enjoyed being mean. Nothing was ever his fault. Everyone around him was treated better at work. He had to work twice as hard to get half the recognition. He complained all the time. Chastised me every chance he got." She paused. "And slept with a lot of other women. When I found out, he informed me it was my fault. If I was the wife he expected and deserved, he wouldn't have to look elsewhere."

"Bullshit. You know he was full of it, right? The term narcissist comes to mind. He would tear you down to make himself feel superior."

She laughed, the sound bitter. "He did it well. He had broken me down for years, constantly belittling me, chipping away at my confidence. Taking away my choices. He was first in everything. But he made one mistake."

"Which was?" I asked, trying to keep my voice calm. I wanted to go find this bastard and beat the shit out of him.

"He made me a mother. Suddenly, I had someone to care for. A little baby I had to protect—one I loved more than anything in the world. I started questioning him. His motives. His thoughts. I hated the pristine, colorless world he forced us to live in. The cold house. The perfect image. He was horrified if he came home and Abby was fussy or messy. He even hated that I called her Abby, not Abigail, which he insisted she be referred to as." She shook her head. "She was too little and sweet for that big name. I called her Abby when he wasn't around. I'd make up songs with her name in them, and she loved them."

She was quiet for a moment, looking thoughtful. "He picked on me all the time. If the house wasn't in perfect order. If I didn't look as if I walked off a runway. But I started fighting back. Arguing with him. Still, he had the upper hand. Everything I had was his. I had no money, no job, no experience. Not even a credit card of my own. I knew if I left, he would find me and bring me back. So, I fought to give Abby a normal life. It was as if I lived two separate lives. During the day, we dressed the way we liked. Went places. Had fun. When he was around, we were shadows. Always perfect."

She stopped, gripping the worktable.

"Did he hit you, Quinn?" I asked, my voice tight.

"No, he used words. They didn't leave marks." She met my worried gaze. "They only leave scars."

I knew what she meant. Unable to take the distance between us, I crossed the room, gathering her hands in mine. "What gave you the courage to walk?"

"Abby. I was tired of watching her light fade when he was around. She was only four and acted like an adult. I didn't want that for her. He ignored us unless it was to yell or demand one of his stupid outings. We'd have to dress up and act like a happy family. There was an event he insisted we go to. Abby wasn't feeling well, but he refused to listen. She wasn't herself—listless and refusing to do as he demanded. We ended up leaving, and when he got home later, he ranted for hours. I told him I was done and wanted a divorce. He refused and we argued. He grabbed me and shook me really hard while yelling. He left bruises because he was holding me so tight and he shook me so roughly I had a headache for hours. It frightened me and I wondered how long until he lost his temper with Abby. How defenseless she would be if he shook her." She swallowed, her voice shaky. "I couldn't take that chance."

I nodded, knowing this was the incident she'd been thinking about the other day. The thought of him hurting her made me furious, but I tamped down my anger so she would keep talking.

"When he left for work on Monday, I went to a lawyer and she helped me. The next week, I was gone. He found me fast, but I had people on my side now. For almost a year, he badgered me. I sold the car he'd given me. The fancy phone. The jewelry. Even most of the expensive clothes he'd insisted I had to wear went to a consignment shop. He was furious, but he'd put things in my name for tax purposes. I lived off that tiny nest egg I accumulated. We stayed in a small place. Took the bus and walked. I had a cheap, throwaway cell. I worked at the local diner. And I hadn't been that happy in a long time. No one was constantly telling me what I was doing wrong. How much I'd let them down, time after time. I had my own thoughts and feelings. Abby could laugh. Scatter her toys. She was happy. I became Quinn again." She tugged on her overall straps. "I wore what I liked, ate what I liked, and lived how I wanted. I rediscovered myself."

I nodded encouragingly. "I like this rediscovered Quinn," I murmured.

She smiled. "I like her too."

"What happened?"

"He met the perfect woman, who was exactly like him. Then he couldn't divorce me fast enough. He signed away his rights and gave me money to get me out of his life." She sighed, her body suddenly slumping. I pulled her into my arms. "We moved here," she murmured, her head resting on my chest.

"Jesus, I regret the way I acted with you," I muttered, holding her tight. "I'll regret that the rest of my life."

"No, you were just you." I felt her smile. "A grump. But I could see you were using it to keep people away, not because you were unkind."

"I will never be a grump with you again."

She tilted her head back, her eyes warm. "I think you're kinda cute when you're being a grump. But I do like the Farmer John Abby knows."

"You know him too. Or at least, you're beginning to."

"I am." She smiled. "I like him."

I bent down, taking her mouth. "He likes you. Very much."

We kissed sweetly. Softly. I drew back. I looked around the kitchen, wanting, needing to explain something to her. "I knew this place well," I began.

"Oh?"

"Thelma Hopkins was a second mother to me even before I lost mine. I ate here a lot. She always helped me make up meals in the spring I could eat during the busy planting season. She'd drop off food from here all the time. Check on me. I could talk to her about everything. When she died, it was as if I lost my mom all over again."

"Oh, John."

"Meatloaf Monday was my favorite. She always made extra for me. I loved it cold on sandwiches." I shrugged ruefully. "The thought of a newcomer arriving and taking over her place didn't sit well with me. I took it out on you, and I'm sorry."

"Yet you supported me at the city council meeting."

"I realized Thelma would kick my ass for being a grump. She would want this diner to be brought back to life. By being an ass, I was dishonoring her."

"So you didn't object about my silly name."

"I love the name. It's exactly right. And I want to kick my own ass for being anything but nice to you."

She cupped my face. "You are forgiven."

"Just like that?"

"I forgave you when you supported my request. And since then, I've grown quite fond of you," she said with a wink.

Unable to resist, I kissed her again.

"Can I help you with something so you can go home?"

"I just have to put the roast in the slow cooker. It'll cook low and slow all night."

"May I come over once I finish for the day? Spend some time with you and Abby?"

"Oh, she would love that!"

"And her momma?"

She linked her arms around my neck. "She'd love that too."

"Good."

After my chores were done, I stopped by the farmhouse, had a shower, and then grabbed a tote I had found when I was looking for clean towels in the hall closet. I put it in the back seat, glancing at the sky. It was beginning to cloud over, and they were calling for rain soon. If it stormed, I would be there with Abby and Quinn. Maybe that would help calm their fears.

I swung by the pizza place, ordering a large pie. I didn't want Quinn to cook, and I had a feeling pizza would be a treat for them. I added some pop and ice cream, putting it in the tote.

I was right, judging from the delight on Abby's face and Quinn's wide smile, even as she protested my bringing food. Unable to resist, I bent and silenced her with a kiss. The soft coo from Abby as I lifted my head made Quinn's eyes widen.

"Farmer John," Abby hush-whispered. "You kissed my momma."

"Yep."

"Are you her boyfriend?"

"Ah—"

Quinn bent down. "That's a personal question, Abby."

"But Momma, he kissed you! In the front yard! It's not like when he kissed you in the kitchen the other day."

I met Quinn's shocked gaze. Obviously, the kid was stealthy, and we were busted.

"Yeah, I'm your momma's boyfriend."

"Okay. I like you." She skipped away. "Let's have pizza!"

"I guess we have her approval," I mused, handing Quinn the box and reaching for the tote.

"You bring pizza, swings, and share your cake. Hardly a shock," Quinn informed me.

"Does Momma approve?" I teased.

"Depends what toppings you put on the pizza. There had better be some olives."

"I got the Kitchen Sink. Basically every topping, but I skipped the hot peppers."

"Then you're a keeper."

I grinned all the way into the house.

After we ate, the rain hit. Growing up, Laura had loved storms. We both had. We'd sit on the porch with our parents, watching the rain dance on the hard ground, the way the wind moved the trees, and we were fascinated watching the lightning light up the sky, eager for the rumble of the thunder that followed.

This wasn't the case with Quinn and Abby. Abby clutched her doll and teddy, looking fearful and upset. Quinn was stronger, but she jumped at the sound of the gathering force of the storm. Quinn had lit some candles in case the power went out. She had some cushions and blankets on the sofa, but I saw the way they were eyeing the hallway to the bedroom.

Not really wanting to sit in a closet, I sat on the floor, patting the space between my open legs. "Quinn—here." Confused, she did as I asked, and then I beckoned to Abby. "Your turn."

She scrambled onto her mother's lap, and I draped a blanket around us and wrapped them in my embrace. "Nothing can hurt you," I assured them. "I have you both."

I felt Quinn relax, and Abby curled up, patting my forearm with her little hand.

"Can you sing, Momma?" she asked, still nervous.

I wasn't prepared for Quinn's voice. She sang softly, one hand sifting through the curls on Abby's head. Her voice was sweet. Lyrical. Rich. I shut my eyes, letting it roll over me, the sound so beautiful I lost myself to it. She sang and hummed, her talent evident.

Outside, the storm began, the rain heavy. The lights went out, but we stayed a huddled little ball of bodies, arms, and legs as Quinn sang. The candlelight flickered on the walls and the wind rattled the windows, but I kept my girls safe. I didn't have to do much. Murmur quiet words of comfort. Press a kiss to Quinn's head. Squeeze Abby's hand that rested on my arm. Praise the song Quinn finished, hoping for another. She sang some old songs, a couple I recognized from the radio and a few cute kid songs, having Abby sing with her.

I enjoyed myself in a way I didn't expect. Protecting them felt good. Holding them felt right. Hearing Quinn sing was incredible. Feeling their trust caused an emotion I hadn't experienced for a long time. Despite the reason for it, it was a heady sensation. One I liked and couldn't recall feeling before. Time passed, the lights coming back on, but still, we sat together.

Quinn fell quiet, and I peered over her shoulder. "She asleep?" I whispered.

"Yes. She never falls asleep in a storm." Quinn tilted her head back, meeting my eyes. "You made her feel safe, John."

"I think your singing did the trick. You have an incredible voice, Quinn. Absolutely beautiful."

"Oh."

"You must know that."

"I always loved to sing. Preston told me my 'warbling' was irksome. When I reminded him that he used to enjoy it, he told me he only said it to be polite."

"Do you have his address?" I asked, my voice mild enough.

"No. I know where he works, but why—" She stopped. "Don't be silly. You're not going to go beat him up."

"I want to. I want to show him how words and fists can feel the same."

Her eyes shone. "No. But I admit, I love that you want to."

"Should we put Pumpkin to bed?"

"Yeah. I have to figure out how."

"Move forward a little."

She did, and I slid out, hauling myself up onto the sofa. Then I stood, stretched and bent, lifting Abby from Quinn's lap. She was easy to hold with one arm, and I held out my hand, pulling Quinn to her feet.

"Good God, you're strong," she muttered.

I followed her down the hall, amused. "I basically work out from morning until night. I hope so."

I set Abby on the bed, watching as Quinn efficiently tucked her in, arranged the doll and teddy, then bent and brushed a kiss to Abby's forehead. "Night, baby," she whispered. "I'll leave the light on."

We tiptoed back to the living room, the night-light casting stars and shimmering moons on the ceiling.

"Will she wake up?"

"No, usually once she's down, that's it. Unless there is another loud storm."

"I think it's passed."

"Good."

I sat on the sofa, pulling Quinn close. She snuggled beside me, her head on my shoulder.

"You okay?" I asked.

"I'm good. Having you here really helped."

I pressed a kiss to her head. "Good, but I meant about earlier. Sharing your story with me."

"Yes. I feel…I don't know, lighter, having shared it."

"That's always a positive."

She was quiet then looked up at me. "That day when you stopped to help me with my tire, you said something."

"I said a lot of stupid things."

"No, I meant you said something that stuck with me. About someone flirting with a stranger and it not being the first time."

"Ah, that."

"That happened to you?" she whispered.

"Yeah. My ex."

She turned, taking my hand. "I'll listen if you want."

I ran my knuckles down her cheek, not really wanting to talk about my past, but knowing she deserved to know my story too.

I blew out a long breath. "I'll keep this short since I don't like thinking about it, never mind talking."

"You don't have to," she offered.

I hunched closer and kissed her. "Yeah, this time, I do."

Maybe I'd feel lighter too.

12

JOHN

I paused, gathering my thoughts. She didn't rush me or ask questions, simply waiting for me to be ready.

"I met Moira at an equipment auction. She was a sales rep, and we talked. I found her attractive, smart. When I was leaving, we bumped into each other, and she gave me her number. I called and asked her out. She lived in Wells, which is another little town close to here."

"I looked there. Not as nice as Richton."

I smiled at her words. I had to agree with her.

"She traveled a lot with her job. Always on the go. She was a no-nonsense person. A real go-getter." I snorted, thinking about it. "A user."

"What happened?"

"She supposedly lived with a friend. I only saw her place once—she liked to come here. She'd be here, then gone, come back, stay a bit, then off she'd go. I understood because I thought it was what she did. I didn't particularly like it, but I knew what I was getting into. Or so I thought."

I scrubbed my hand over my face. "Before I knew it, she was basically living here. Lots of her things were at the farmhouse. When she was around, we hung around Richton. She worked remotely, and I managed the farm. Things seemed great, and the truth was, I was falling hard for her."

Quinn shifted a little, and I squeezed her leg. "I'm trying to be honest. Does it upset you?"

"No, I have a feeling where this is going, and I don't like it."

"Laura didn't like her, which caused a few issues. Laura saw things I either didn't see or refused to see. Things that didn't make sense. A few times, her story didn't line up. I noticed she had more than one phone. She insisted one was work and one was personal, and I accepted that. But she was lying about that and a whole lot more."

"She was married?" Quinn guessed.

"Yep. And playing me well." I had to get up and walk. I kissed Quinn's hand and paced the room. "She had a husband and another life a few towns over. Wells was her base—her friend knew what she was doing and didn't care. She lived two lives. I found out her goal with me was to get at my money, drain as much as she could, and disappear. Go back to her other life until she found another idiot. Rinse and repeat."

"How awful."

"She used people. Any way she could, the whole time acting like a good person and fooling everyone. She said all the right things. Acted the way she thought I wanted her to act."

"Laura saw through her."

"Yep."

I sat down beside her. "I was stupidly thinking she was the one. I even started to think about marrying her one day."

She grasped my hand. "Oh, John." She worried her bottom lip. "How did you find out?"

"It was a fluke. I was helping Bob again. I went to Wells to pick up something for him. I was sitting in my truck, and I saw Moira with another man, getting into a car. She was supposed to be on a business trip, and instantly, I knew something was really wrong. I followed them to a house a few towns away, and I took down the address. I gave it to a friend I know who does some investigation work, and he found out a whole lot of information. She was married. There had been others like me. Findlay was her maiden name. She liked to pick her 'boyfriends' from her job." I laughed without humor. "She had access to my personal profile. My banking. Anyone who was looking to be part of the auctions her company ran. She picked out the best prospects. Or at least, that was what she told me when I confronted her."

"That must have been terrible."

"I saw the real her. Luckily, it blew up before she took anything much from me. But it was ugly. She had a lot to say about me. None of it particularly flattering."

"She broke your heart."

"She shattered my trust."

"Then you thought I was doing the same thing."

I shook my head. "A huge mistake on my part. I know you're different. You're real. You didn't contrive to meet me. You're not after me for my bank account or to relieve the boredom of being married."

"That's what she said?" Quinn asked, horrified.

"Yeah, she liked to walk on the wild side and top up her bank account. Apparently, I was even more boring than her husband, but I was a decent fuck." I shrugged at Quinn's startled expression. "She'd thought I'd be rougher."

Quinn's eyes widened. "I sec."

I realized she was still confused, and I sighed. "When I was twenty-two, I won the lottery. Not a huge amount—just over a hundred thousand. But instead of spending it, I invested it. I had my finance guy take some risks that paid off, and we doubled it. Then I stashed it in various places—some high-risk, some not. I invested in real estate. I'm not rich, but I have a good solid nest egg. Cody's education will be paid for. That was my gift to my sister."

"You always put family first."

I nodded in agreement.

"But she saw that large amount, plus the money from the houses, and thought she should have some of it. Most of it, if she had her way. Pretend to marry me and get access to the accounts. Drain them and walk." I barked out another laugh. "She didn't expect to be found out, and she had no idea how hard it would be to get at the money. She walked away with nothing but a few things I gave her and some cash I kept on hand. Her husband found out what she was doing, and he divorced her. Last I heard, she'd moved to Toronto. Changed careers since there aren't a lot of farmers living in the big city. I feel sorry for whatever business she chooses and whoever she sinks her claws into next."

"I'm sorry you went through that."

"I think we both struck out with our exes." I took her hands, kissing the inside of her wrist. "But that's in the past, and we're looking forward now, together. Right?"

"Yes."

Then she crawled into my lap, looping her arms around my neck. "You're not boring. I find you intelligent and interesting. Funny." She winked. "Even when you're being a grump."

I laughed. "Good to know. I live a simple life, Quinn. It's what I know. What I'm comfortable with."

"That's what I want too," she replied. "A simple life. That doesn't mean boring. It means being happy, surrounding myself with the people I care about, and enjoying the world around me. Money doesn't buy happiness. If anything, my marriage taught me that. For all the money Preston has, I don't think he's ever been happy since he started accumulating it. Being rich was his goal, but somewhere along the way, he forgot to live."

I pulled her closer. "So you wanna try not being boring with me for a while?"

She pressed her mouth to mine. "Yes."

I kissed her, groaning as our tongues slid together in a slow, sensuous dance. She buried herself tighter, her grip on my neck tightening. I slipped my hand under her shirt, tracing her spine, smiling as she shivered. I dropped my hands to her ass, cupping the cheeks and grinding against her. I felt her heat through the material that separated us, and I knew she'd be wet for me.

I pulled back, my breathing fast. Our gazes locked, and she licked her lips.

"You don't kiss as if you're just a decent fuck," she whispered. "I think you'll make me forget my name." She ground against me. "And I want you to show me."

My cock was hard as marble, her dirty confession echoing in my mind.

I gazed down the hall. "Does Abby wake up a lot?"

"No."

"You really want this? Want me?"

She buried her face into my neck, kissing and biting at my skin. "Yes."

I stood. "Then hang on, baby. I'll remind you of your name later. Not that it'll matter. All you'll have to remember is that you're mine."

I carried her to her bed, laying her down. I pushed the door closed behind me, then turned to look at her. Her dark hair was spread over the pillow, her lips swollen and her gaze warm. Sultry. Focused on me.

She sat up, then pulled her shirt over her head. She wasn't wearing anything else, and her breasts were full and tempting, the nipples pink and hard, begging for my mouth. My teeth.

I yanked my shirt over my head, dropping it on the floor. In one swift motion, I undid my jeans, pushing them off my hips. My erection tented the front of my boxers as I kicked away my pants and stared at her. I crossed the room, pausing by the edge of the bed, then leaned on my hands, caging her between them as I kissed her. I balanced on one hand, pulling her close with my other. She arched her back, her chest pressing into mine. She was soft and warm against my rougher skin, the delicate bones of her back melding to my hand. I kissed her until she began to tremble, gripping my shoulders and pleading my name quietly. I laid her down and, in one move, stripped her shorts off, revealing her to my eyes. For a moment, she looked panicked until I shook my head. "You are so incredibly beautiful, Quinn. I can't wait to taste every inch of you. Feel you wrapped around me."

She looked worried, and I frowned. "What is it?"

"Um, aside from my ex, I don't have a lot of experience. And he said—"

I cut her off. "His opinion counts for nothing. I don't want to know what he said because I don't care since it was no doubt a lie," I stated fiercely. "It's you and me now. I think you're beautiful. I know we're going to be amazing together. Trust me?"

"Yes."

I lifted her foot and kissed the ankle. "Then relax. It's just us."

"I like us."

I fell to my knees, pulling her close. "So do I."

QUINN

I didn't plan on the night ending up with John in my bedroom, kneeling in front of me. I was nervous and shaking, but after a few moments, the nerves were replaced by something else entirely. John kissed his way up my legs, pausing behind my knees to tease and taste. He did the same by my thighs. Then he kissed my stomach, ghosting his lips over the stretch marks I'd gotten while pregnant. "Pumpkin kisses," he whispered. "Adorable."

Preston had informed me they were unsightly and urged me to try to have them removed. He'd even booked me an appointment and had been upset when he'd found out they could be lessened but not erased. It didn't really matter since he hadn't touched me once I was pregnant anyway.

John's reaction to them made me smile. From now on, I would think of them as Pumpkin kisses.

I gasped as he lowered his head, using his thumbs to open me to his mouth. He teased me, trailing his tongue slowly, circling my clit but not touching it.

"So wet," he praised. "All for me."

I groaned when he closed his mouth around me, licking and sucking. The sensation was intense. He lapped and bit. Blew warm air across the top to tease, ran his finger over me in gentle passes until I begged for more, then slid his finger inside, rubbing me hard with his thumb. My body erupted with pleasure when he added a second finger then took me back into his mouth, his tongue doing things that should be illegal. I rolled my hips, trying to get closer. Needing more. Needing everything he would give me. I had never experienced sensations like that. It was as if small bombs were going off in my body, detonating at different times. I gasped and begged. Called his name. Gripped at his hair.

Then my orgasm hit me. I arched my back, a low moan escaping my throat. Everything locked down as wave after wave of pleasure hit me. The small bombs

I had been feeling became a boatload of dynamite, exploding and sending me skyrocketing.

Then John was over me, his cock buried deep inside. He was big, thick, and hard. He moved in powerful thrusts, lifting my hips and hitting me in a place I never knew existed. I gripped his forearms, gasping his name. "John. *Please. I can't.*"

"You can and you will. You're going to come all over me." He lifted me higher. "I won't last long, baby. It's been a while, and I want you too much. So you're gonna come with me, and later, I'll take my time. You hear me?" he growled out in a voice I'd never heard. It was sexy. Demanding. In charge.

"Oh God," I whispered, covering my mouth as I felt my body beginning to take over. I wanted to scream, but if I did, I would wake Abby.

"That's it, Quinn. Feel it. Feel me." He grinned, his expression intense. "I'm going to fuck you into oblivion, and then we'll start over."

His words crashed over me, and I fell again. I was aware of his grip tightening, his low, guttural noises, and I felt the rush of his release deep inside me. I opened my eyes, watching him succumb. The cords on his neck were tight as he threw his head back. His eyes were shut as he grunted and moaned my name. He kept moving, drawing out his pleasure and mine.

And then he froze, still holding me tight, heaving out a long, satisfied sigh.

He opened his eyes, our gazes locking. Tenderly, he pulled out, and my body protested his absence. "You all right?" he asked. He looked down, frowned, and stepped back. "*Holy shit*, I was so carried away, I didn't… We didn't…"

"I'm on birth control," I assured him. "And I haven't since before Abby was born."

He looked startled, then cupped my cheek. "It's been a long time for me as well. And I was checked."

"Me too."

"I'll get some condoms tomorrow, though."

I felt my blush. "Okay."

We snuck to the bathroom, cleaning up, then back to my room. We snuggled for a while, talking quietly. We didn't bring up our pasts or anything heavy. We shared a few stories, opening up a little more to each other. "Do you want more kids?" he asked.

"Yes." I swallowed, worried about his answer. "Do you?"

"A houseful."

"Oh."

"Do you see yourself settling here, Quinn?" he asked. "For good?"

I peered up at him, seeing that vulnerability again on his face. "I like it here a lot. Especially now. I have no plans on leaving."

"Especially now?" he teased. "Because you painted the house?"

I giggled. "No, because my landlord is walking sex on legs and likes my cooking."

He nipped my neck. "That's not the only thing he likes." He kissed me again, pulling me tight to his chest. My heart began to race, and desire swept over me. I wanted him again.

He eased back, pressing his forehead to mine. His breathing was heavy.

"I guess I'd better not risk staying the night."

I felt the flash of disappointment even though I knew he was right. "Probably."

"If I don't go soon, I won't be able to tear myself away from you."

I peered up at him. "Really?"

His kiss was soft and sweet this time. "Really."

"How about I come to the farmhouse and make dinner tomorrow?"

"How about you come to the farmhouse, and I'll grill. You cook all day."

"You work too."

"We'll make it together."

"Deal."

He rolled from bed, pulling on his clothes. I wrapped a robe around me, following him to the door. He turned, drawing me into his arms and kissing me until I had trouble breathing. He stepped back, looking regretful. "Tomorrow," he promised as he opened the door.

"John?" I murmured, waiting until he met my eyes. "That was more than decent. I'd give you an A."

A wicked grin crossed his face, and he smirked, shutting the door behind him. Before I could stop him, he swung me into his arms, heading back down the hall. In my room, he tossed me onto the bed.

"A?" he said, sounding disgusted. "I'm not leaving until I get an A fucking plus. So, get ready, baby. It's gonna be a long night."

Then he was on me.

And I was good with that.

13

JOHN

I pulled on my pants, then yanked my shirt over my head. I hesitated at the foot of Quinn's bed, looking at her in the semi-darkness. It was just after four, and I had woken after a brief period of sleep with her. Otherwise, we'd been at it all night.

Unplanned. Unprotected. Unusual.

Perfection.

She was everything I could have dreamed of in a lover. Loving, responsive, giving, sexy. Any misgivings her ex had left her with vanished as the moments went by. She became more vocal, pleading, leading instead of following. I'd had her three times, the last one as she rode me, her long hair wild around her face, her nails scoring my skin as she drove herself, and me, to completion. She was stunning in her passion. Watching her orgasm, feeling her body spasm, tighten around me, was the most erotic vision I had ever seen.

I was loath to leave her, but I knew I had to. Pumpkin would be awake soon, and she would ask questions. Lots of questions. The entire community would be up when the sun broke through the dawn, and my truck wasn't exactly quiet. Although we were adults, I felt an underlying need to protect Quinn and Abby from as much gossip as possible.

I bent and brushed a final kiss to Quinn's forehead, my lips lingering on her warm skin. She smelled of her light perfume, of me, of us.

I liked it.

I made my way through the silent house, peeking in on Abby, then letting myself out. And after making sure the door locked behind me, I headed to my truck. I was glad Quinn's house was so close to the corner as I started the engine and left. That meant fewer people looking out to see what vehicle was around.

I had another long, busy day ahead of me, and I needed to get back to the farm and begin the never-ending list of chores that waited.

Yet somehow, the thoughts of the two females I'd left behind lingered on my mind all day.

The sun was high in the sky when I headed back to the house. The crops were coming along well, and I had finished the repairs to the fence the donkey had damaged. I did some plowing in a new section of land I had added last year but not cultivated yet. I was going to experiment with a different crop and see how it did before using the other half of the land. I was tired and my body ached. I had a slight headache from the heat and the fact that I hadn't drunk nearly enough water as I'd been too busy. The sandwiches I'd eaten early were nowhere near as good as the ones I'd eaten from the Dill. I laughed quietly as I rounded the corner. Even I was calling it that now.

I stopped in surprise, seeing Quinn's SUV in the driveway. I wasn't expecting her until later. I had pulled some steaks from the freezer, but that was as far as I had gotten with any ideas for dinner. I sped up, climbing the steps and walking into the house.

Two things hit me. The incredible aroma of something cooking, and the laughter of Quinn and Abby coming from the kitchen. Both were foreign occurrences for me. I was used to an empty house— and silence.

But they made me smile, and I strode forward, spying my girls at the counter, making cookies.

The thought caught me off guard. *My girls.* I repeated the words in my head. I liked how they sounded.

I paused and watched them, their heads so close it was impossible to tell where one ended and the other began, the way their dark hair wove together. The air was rife with the scent of chocolate and sugar. A large bowl of potato salad sat to one side, making my mouth water. I saw the steaks resting in marinade and a large pile of skewered fresh vegetables ready to join them on the grill.

"You know," I drawled. "I could call the local constable and have you ladies arrested for break and enter."

They looked up, surprised. That turned to delight when Abby grinned widely. "Farmer John!" she crowed. "We're making cookies!"

I pushed off the doorframe. "I can smell them." I snuck one, popping it into my mouth and chewing. "Delicious."

I met Quinn's eyes and, unable to stop myself, looped an arm around her waist and pulled her in. Remembering Abby, I pressed a kiss to Quinn's cheek. "Hey."

She pulled back, her cheeks flushing. "Hey, yourself." Then she tossed her hair. "You can't have us arrested since we were given a key."

I lifted my eyebrows. "Is that a fact?"

She nodded in triumph. "Yes. Laura gave it to me."

I bent and pressed a kiss to Abby's head, stroking her soft hair and winking at her. "And how did you accomplish that?"

Quinn grinned. "Bribing her with dinner."

I looked around, suddenly understanding the amount of food being prepped. "Ah."

"She's bringing some chicken skewers to add to the protein portion. She offered me the key so we could come and get started. She said you wouldn't mind..." Quinn trailed off, looking nervous.

Abby was busy rolling a ball of dough for the cookie tray, and I quickly pressed a hard kiss to Quinn's full mouth. "I don't mind at all," I assured her. "Except for the fact that I have to share you."

"Stop it," she murmured.

"What time are they coming?"

"About an hour."

"Okay, I'm going to go shower so I don't smell like dust, dirt, and cows."

Abby wrinkled her nose. "Eww."

She squealed with laughter as I hoisted her into the air and blew a raspberry on her stomach. "Careful," I warned. "Or I'll put you in the field, and you'll be all smelly too."

She kept laughing, and I set her down, heading to the door. I looked over my shoulder at the sight.

My girls in my kitchen. My family coming to join us.

What a great day.

"Tell me more about John as a kid," Quinn urged, laughter glinting in her eyes.

"I think you've heard enough," I said dryly, sipping my beer and shaking my head at my sister, who was enjoying herself.

Far too much, in my opinion.

Quinn and Abby had heard about my attempt to help my gramps plant seeds. How I had decided one wasn't enough in a hole and put in about a dozen—of different types of seeds.

"Gramps spent hours trying to thin out the plants and fix them," *Laura said, laughing. "John also decided plants needed more water than Gramps thought, so he drowned half the crop before Gramps got to him."*

Laura ignored me. She leaned over, her amusement

high as she spoke to Quinn. "When he was young, he got a bike."

"Like Cody," Abby piped up.

Laura nodded. "He was a bit younger and the bike was used, but he spent hours painting it and shining it up. He was so excited, and he was going to the cliff to show it off to his friends."

I groaned. "Not this."

"What happened?" Quinn asked, resting her elbow on the table and grinning.

Bob caught my eye and lifted one shoulder as if to say, "Give it up, man. No point fighting it."

He was right, so I sat back and took another sip of my beer.

"Have you been to the cliff in the park?" Laura asked, her eyes dancing.

"No," Quinn replied. "I haven't."

"Cliff is a suggestive word," I muttered. "More like a bluff."

Laura and Bob laughed. "Now. Back then, it seemed huge." Laura turned to Quinn. "The water is fairly shallow along the beach. By the cliff, there's a drop off into the water, and at that point, it's much deeper. When we were kids, you'd dare someone to jump—it was a big thing."

"I see."

"Anyway, another big thing was to pedal your bike really fast toward the cliff, then turn before you got there, hitting your brakes hard. The one closest to the edge of the cliff won."

"What was the prize?" Quinn asked.

"Bragging rights," I interjected. "When I was a kid, that was the biggest deal."

"Shut up, John. I'm telling the story," Laura demanded.

I held up my hands in supplication.

"Anyway, John had taken the bike apart and put it back together, making some adjustments. He was sure he'd win. He rode it to the cliff and challenged Craig, who was the current 'reigning champ.' But John hadn't quite tightened everything as well as he should…" She paused dramatically. "As he barreled toward the cliff, the handlebars came off. He went one way, and the bike took off, sailing through the air like a glider. Over the cliff and through the air a long way before sinking into the lake." She smirked. "Even John stood and watched it."

"It was impressive," I admitted with a sheepish shrug. "I had no idea it could fly like that."

"Oh my," Quinn said, trying to hold in a laugh.

"I remember wondering if I was bleeding enough that my dad would sympathize, or if he'd whoop my butt for being so stupid."

Abby's eyes went wide. "Oh no! You were bleeding? Farmer John, were you killed?"

Laughing, I swung her up on my knee. "Nope." I pulled up my shirt sleeve. "But I got this scar." Then I touched my eyebrow. "And this one, plus a big one on my knee. The bike sank, and we never recovered it."

"Oh no," Quinn murmured.

"My dad decided that, plus more chores, would be my punishment. And I had to go back to my old bike. I didn't get a new one for a year." I laughed. "I think Dad only relented 'cause I had a growth spurt and I kept hitting my knees on the handlebars, and Mom nagged him all the time."

"Any more cliff races?" Quinn asked.

"Nope. I learned my lesson. Next time I went to the cliff was to make out with Jenny Stait."

"What's make out?" Abby asked.

"Oh, um, we snuggled."

"Oh, like you did with Momma last night in her bed?"

The entire room became silent.

"What?" Quinn asked, her voice an octave higher. "You mean when we were sitting together during the storm, right?"

"No, Momma." Abby shook her head, impatient. "Later. I woke up in my bed and I came to see you, but you and Farmer John were snuggling in your bed. I knew you were okay, so I went back to my bed." She smiled. "You were having a sleepover!"

For a moment, I couldn't find my voice. We thought we'd been so careful. I hadn't heard Abby get up. Or the bedroom door open. I had been too exhausted from fucking her mother for hours.

What if she'd gotten up while—

I couldn't bring myself to finish the thought or the consequences it would have brought.

Cody unwittingly saved the day. "Oh—ha-ha-ha," he laughed. "Uncle John does that. He sometimes tucks me in and falls asleep too! Remember last time, Uncle J? You rolled off my bed, and you never even woke up."

Everyone laughed, the relief on Quinn's face evident.

Cody leaned his elbows on the table. "When Uncle J took me to Toronto last year for my birthday, there was only one bed in the room, and we shared it. He didn't fall off 'cause it was, like, the biggest bed I've ever seen, but he snored."

I shook my head. "I was tired, bud. You wore me out."

"What did you do there?" Quinn asked.

"We went to a baseball game and the aquarium," Cody told her. "And the coolest restaurant where I could see everything. It was the best day ever!"

"The CN Tower," I explained. "He wanted to see a game. I thought the aquarium would be cool. We looked around in the morning, had lunch at the CN Tower, the aquarium in the afternoon, and a baseball game in the evening. We were both exhausted."

"That sounds like fun."

"Did you ever go? Since you lived there?" Laura asked.

Quinn looked sad. "No." She glanced at Abby, who was busy chatting with Cody. "My, ah, ex didn't do 'fun' things. Our schedule was pretty set."

"Well, maybe you can one day." Laura looked at me meaningfully, and I nodded slightly in her direction. It was a good idea I would have to think about. I was grateful, though, that Cody's story had shifted the focus off Quinn and me and our "sleepover."

"Maybe," Quinn said with a smile.

Laura and Quinn insisted on clearing the table. Bob fell asleep on the sofa, and I headed outside, hearing the kids laughing. I crossed the yard, going to the back. Cody was pushing Abby in the old tire swing I had put up for him years before. She was laughing as she soared, but my heart hit my throat when I saw how high. I hurried forward, waving at him to stop.

"What, Uncle J? She's having fun."

"I know. I haven't checked the rope lately."

"Oh, okay." He stopped pushing her and the wide arc of the swing stopped, but Abby kept pumping her legs. It kept her going, but not as high.

"She's a girl," I explained quietly. "Smaller than you. Younger. You have to look out for her."

"I know. I was watching. I didn't think about the rope, though." He peered up. "Looks okay."

I followed his line of vision. The rope was thick and still strong. "Still, you gotta be careful."

He snorted. "Abby is tough. She's not like other girls. She fell earlier and didn't even whine about it. Just brushed off her pants and kept going. I like her." He paused. "Is she my cousin?"

I scratched my chin. "Pardon?"

"When you marry her mom, will she be my cousin? 'Cause I gotta stand up for her and all if she is family."

"You should, even as a friend."

He gave me a look. "I will. But family is even more important."

"I just started dating her mom. We're not talking marriage yet."

Even as the words were out of my mouth, I found my gaze straying over to the kitchen window, where I could see Quinn and Laura working in the kitchen. I wondered what it would be like to come home to Quinn daily. To sit across from her and Abby and listen to them tell me about their days. To be able to tell them about mine.

How it would feel to end the day lying beside Quinn in our bed.

There definitely would be sleepovers of the adult variety.

I shook my head to clear it of the strange thoughts. It was way too soon for that.

Cody shrugged. "If you like her, you should think about it, Uncle J. She's pretty, and I heard Jay's dad say he was gonna ask her out. He said he's looking for a replacement something."

I had to hold in my derision. Jay's dad was looking for wife number three to cook, clean, and be a mother to his hell-raising kids. That wasn't happening.

I'd make sure of it.

I'd seen his truck at the Dill a few times early in the day when I was in town.

I decided tomorrow might be a good day to try Quinn's breakfast.

Earlier than usual the next morning, I finished my chores, leaving it to the men I hired to complete the watering and checking of the crops. I showered and headed into town, pulling up on the main street. I huffed out a huge breath. Our little town had one salon and barber, a drugstore, the hardware and garden, and a surprisingly decent grocery store that had an in-store butcher, which was rare these days.

The liquor store was small but adequate, and right beside it was the florist. It had been around since I was a child, the current owner's mother having worked there, and her mother before that. I knew the woman who ran it, having gone to school with her son. Still, I dreaded going in.

I had never bought flowers before in my life, aside from a few bouquets for my mother.

This was new to me. I slid from the truck, entering the florist shop, hoping no one spotted me. Inside was filled with bushes, shrubs, and buckets of flowers. There were plants and pots hanging from the ceiling, in the windows, and perched everywhere. I could smell the flowers, their scent tickling my nose.

A woman came around the back counter. "Morning!" She stopped, seeing me. "John?" she questioned. "John Elliott?"

"Hey, Martha," I greeted her, pushing my baseball hat back. "How are you?"

"Good. I'm good. I'm surprised to see you in here." She clapped her hands. "What are you needing?" Then she frowned. "Is Laura sick?"

"No, she's fine."

She bustled forward. "Oh, that's good. Did you anger her? You need flowers to say you're sorry? I have some funny balloons we can add. They'll make her smile, I guarantee you!"

"They, ah, aren't for Laura."

She stopped, then a wide smile split her face. Her eyes crinkled and danced. "Oh, *romantic* flowers?"

"Um, have a great day sort of flowers," I replied, wishing I'd gone to Mitchell or another little town.

"O…kay," she drawled. "What did you have in mind?"

"No idea. Something bright, maybe?"

"What does she like? Any allergies?"

I blinked. Who knew buying flowers involved so many details. "Look, Martha, I don't know. Can you make me up a nice bouquet that smells good and looks… impressive? Noticeable."

She tapped her chin. "In a vase or out?"

I frowned. What were the chances Quinn had a vase at the restaurant?

"In."

"Gimme ten," she said. "And by impressive, you mean about a hundred bucks or so?"

"Will that be noticeable?"

"From anywhere in the room. No matter how big."

"Perfect."

Twenty minutes later, I carried a large vase of flowers into Kind of a Big Dill. Part of me wished I'd had them delivered, but then I wouldn't be able to make my point.

I saw Jay's truck parked out front, and I decided the looks and smirks I was getting were worth it. He was about to find out Quinn was unavailable.

Inside, the restaurant was busy. Jay was at the counter, sipping a coffee, eating toast. I withheld my snort. Cheap prick. Of course he chose the lowest-priced item on the menu. He was notoriously...*frugal*. A good-looking bastard and, from what I had heard, charming at first, but once the shine wore off, he was simply looking for free maid and child-rearing services.

He saw me, frowning at the sight of the flowers in my arms. I set them on the counter, swinging onto a stool at the end where Quinn had to notice me. I ignored Jay.

A moment later, the kitchen door swung open, and Tammy walked out, her hands full. She eyed up the flowers, then me, a grin crossing her face, but she didn't say anything. She delivered the plates to the table, then returned, pouring me a cup of coffee.

"The boss will be out in a moment. She was just putting more pies in to bake." She eyed the flowers. "If you were hoping to make her smile, you might just have done it."

I frowned, wondering why Quinn was having a bad day. She came out of the kitchen, looking perturbed, but her expression changed when she saw me. Her eyes widened in surprise, and she smiled, the agitation disappearing. When she saw the flowers, she stopped, her smile growing wider, disbelief written on her face.

She stopped in front of me. "John Elliott," she breathed, touching a rose petal. "What have you done?"

At the other end of the counter, Jay's voice was an unwelcome interruption. "Hey, Quinn sweetie, I really need more coffee."

She shut her eyes, then exhaled. Turning her head toward him, she spoke clearly, her voice dripping with sweetness. "You've had five cups, Jay. The last two you let go cold, and I threw them out."

"Bottomless cups," he said snidely.

"If you drink them, not throw them away. Order a real breakfast, and I might give you a fresh one. And for the last time, stop calling me sweetie. We don't know each other well enough for nicknames." She paused. "And we never will."

Tammy came through the door, carrying a pot. "Tammy, I need—" Jay began.

"Not happening, Jay. I heard the boss. Order something besides toast tomorrow." Then Tammy tossed her head and headed away to refill other coffee cups.

Quinn turned to me. Her unanswered question hung between us. Maybe claiming her in public wasn't the best plan. "To make you smile," I offered lamely.

Shock wasn't the right word as she rose up on her toes, gripped the lapels of my flannel shirt and hauled my ass off the stool, dragged me partway over the counter, and kissed me.

Hard.

Passionately.

Way more possessively than I had planned to kiss her.

Then she let me go, and I dropped back onto my stool.

I'd had no idea she was that strong. I had to admit, it was a turn-on.

It seemed as if *I* had just been claimed.

A few people chuckled. Jay stood, muttering about the diner in the next town and left, slamming the door behind him. Tammy walked past and winked. "Way to go, boss lady." She winked. "Nice form, John Elliott. Your butt looks great in those jeans."

Quinn looked cool and calm. But her mouth was red and wet from my tongue. Unable to stop myself, I rose, cupping the back of her head and kissing her back. Then I sat back, grinning at her.

"Tit for tat," I muttered.

She bent close, pouring me more coffee. "And as far as I'm concerned, to be continued."

"Six?"

"My place," she replied and walked away. She stopped, turned, and smiled. "Thanks, John. I love the flowers. Breakfast is on the house."

She winked. "So am I," she mouthed.

I looked down at the counter, grinning. Six o'clock couldn't come quickly enough.

14

QUINN

I locked the door of the restaurant, turning to look at the space. As usual, the staff had everything ready for the morning. Tammy had worked an extra shift, and I had to admit, I loved it when she did. I never had to ask or explain. She knew exactly what to do and how I liked things.

My eyes caught the arrangement sitting beside the cash register. The bright colors and beautiful flowers had been commented on all day by customers and staff. Every chance I got, I stopped and admired them. They were as unexpected as the man who had gifted them to me and as beautiful as his soul.

Not that I would ever tell him that. He'd turn all shades of red, mutter something about men not being beautiful, and look embarrassed. He'd huff and puff and shake his head.

But he was beautiful—on the inside as well as out.

Never, even when we were young and, I thought, in love, had Preston ever bought me flowers. When Abby was born, I had looked around the room, seeing the other women being given gifts by their husbands or partners. Preston had walked in, stared down at the sweet face of our daughter, and muttered that he would have preferred a boy. Then he'd set down the bag he'd forgotten earlier, informed me he had an important meeting to go to, and left.

He did the same the day he brought me home, leaving me alone with a newborn baby, zero clues on what to do, and telling me he'd be late for dinner.

Given I'd had a difficult birth, I told him I wouldn't be cooking. His response had said it all.

"Don't think you can milk this baby thing forever."

I knew then my marriage was over. But it had taken me years to get away.

I drifted toward the flowers, sitting in front of them, tracing the edge of the petals with my finger.

John Elliott.

He was the exact opposite of Preston. Outwardly grumpy, inside a marshmallow. Preston was charming —he said and did all the right things, but inside, he was rotting like an apple that fell from the tree.

John was kind and loving. Sexy in a rough, masculine way. Preston looked like he stepped off a runway, but when you glanced at his eyes, you knew he was empty inside.

I suppressed a shiver, remembering his cold gaze.

John was open and honest with his feelings— especially when he cared for you.

And in bed, he was giving, sexy, and loving. Rough and gentle at the same time. I felt safe with him. I couldn't question his desire. It was evident in his words and on his face, never mind the way he showed me with his body. Simply thinking of how many times he'd brought me to orgasm last night made me blush. Preston had always been more concerned with his pleasure and not mine, and, more times than not, I had none. With John, that was not the case.

I wasn't sure what made me kiss him the way I did in front of everybody. He had looked so unsure suddenly, as if bringing me flowers had displeased me, when it was the opposite. I was thrilled. Touched. And I had to kiss him to show him.

And I hadn't liked the way Mary Jones was eyeing him from the corner. As if he was a prize hunk of beef.

Which he was.

But he was my prize hunk of beef, and I needed her, and everyone else, to know that.

Where the possessiveness had appeared from, I had no idea, but one thing I knew for sure—John hadn't objected to it at all. He'd seemed surprised and delighted by my actions.

I looked at the mirror lining the back wall, studying my reflection. I looked different. Tired, yes, but relaxed. Happy. The frown lines I was used to seeing, the anxiety I carried all the time, were absent.

And I knew it was mostly thanks to the gruff, rough teddy bear of a man who gave me these flowers.

I slipped off the stool and headed to the kitchen. I knew exactly how to thank him.

JOHN

I walked into Quinn's place, using the back door. It felt oddly right to stride into her house without knocking, instead simply calling for her.

"Quinn—I'm here!"

Fast little feet headed my way, and I felt my smile

getting wide. Abby raced around the corner, her dark hair flying behind her. "Farmer John!"

I bent and scooped her up in my arms, kissing her cheek. She grabbed my face, squeezing my cheeks tightly. "Momma said you were coming."

"Here I am," I said in a high voice. "But my face is trapped."

She let out a long string of girlish giggles, releasing her hands. "That's me doing that!"

"Wow. That's a relief."

I set her down as Quinn appeared. She was wearing her denim overalls, and a pale-yellow T-shirt. Bright-pink toenails glinted in the light as her bare feet hit the hardwood floor.

"Hi," she said, looking almost shy.

I leaned down, looping an arm around her waist and tugging her close. I dropped a fast kiss to her lips. "Hi, yourself." I inhaled deeply. "Something smells incredible." I sniffed again. "Is that peach cobbler I smell?"

She grinned. "A birdie named Laura might have mentioned it's your favorite."

I groaned. "Woman, you have no idea."

"It's ginormous," Abby crowed. "Momma said you eat like a horse!"

"Oh, um," Quinn stammered. "I mean—"

I laughed, burying my face into her neck. "I do like to eat delicious things." I grazed my mouth over her ear. "You were the most delicious thing until now. But the smell of your cobbler is giving that memory a run for its money."

She blinked, stepping back. "Well, I suppose you'll have to have a refresher, then, won't you?"

I winked. "Quinn darlin', I look forward to it."

I looked down at my plate in amazement. "Is this…?" I trailed off, my voice catching.

Quinn looked pleased and shy at my reaction. "I found an old cookbook in the cupboard at the restaurant last week. Handwritten recipes and this meatloaf had a big star in the corner. I was hoping it was the one you loved."

I took a bite, chewing and swallowing. "It's perfect."

"I found lots of little notes in the book. I was thinking of doing Throwback Thursdays as an homage to Thelma," she explained. "Feature one of her daily specials every week."

I swallowed around the thickness in my throat. "That would be fabulous. She'd have loved that."

Quinn tasted her dinner and hummed in pleasure. "This will be the first one. This meatloaf is incredible."

"It is."

She smiled. "Good thing, since I made an extra one for you. For sandwiches."

I squeezed her hand. "Now you're talking."

The rest of the meal was filled with chatter from Abby. I sat back with a groan after I finished my third plate. "Good God, you can cook." I winked. "Explains the restaurant thing."

Quinn laughed. "It's more of an eatery or a diner, I think. It's not fancy, and to me, the word restaurant conjures up fancy."

I drained my glass of water, eyeing the last piece of meatloaf on the platter. I had eaten four, so five was probably too many. Quinn saw my gaze and laughed. "Eat it up. You've worked hard today."

"So have you."

"In a different way, yes."

I couldn't resist. The meatloaf was delicious and exactly as I remembered. Bursting with flavor and like a memory come to life. I bit and chewed, swallowing before I spoke again. "You can call your place anything you want. Bottom line is everyone, including my stubborn a—" I cleared my throat "—butt, thinks it's awesome."

She smiled, looking mischievous. "So happy you changed your mind."

Abby looked at me, one eye closed. "You were going to say ass."

I choked around my mouthful. "Ah…"

"I know what that is. I know lots of bad words, but Momma says I can't use them. You were very polite to stop," she informed me. "Ass isn't as bad because it's short for donkey, but we don't say it in public."

I bit back my grin. "You're right, Pumpkin."

She nodded. "Momma, can I be excused until dessert? I need to check my dolls."

"Of course, baby."

Abby wiped her mouth, placing her napkin on the table and sliding off the chair. I heard her run down the short hall, then start talking to her dolls.

"She is very grown up."

Quinn sighed. "Preston demanded it."

"He was hard on the two of you."

"He was. But if that's all she took away from our time with him, I'm glad. She acts more like a little girl now instead of a small adult. I love hearing her laugh. It took a long time before she felt free enough to do so."

"And you?"

"It took me a long time to smile again and really mean it." She stood, picking up her plate, then stopping by my chair. She bent and pressed a sweet kiss to my forehead. "You have helped a lot with that."

"You've done the same."

She opened the oven door. "Well then, Mr. Elliott, I'm about to blow your world wide open. When you taste this peach cobbler, you won't stop smiling for days."

"Where'd you get the peaches?"

"Clingstone Farms. I couldn't believe they had some already."

"Everything is early this year."

"I bought a huge basket of tomatoes too. I decided BLTs were on the menu. I bought some local seven-grain bread, and with my homemade mayo and the pepper bacon I did, we sold out by one."

"Awesome."

"I want to do that," she said as she scooped the cobbler into bowls. She lifted her eyebrow at me in a silent question after two large spoonfuls. I shook my head, and with a grin, she added more.

"Do what?"

"More farm to table. Make a special with what I get that day or week. Fresh produce, homemade goods from the locals. Feature them. We don't get a lot of tourists, but today, I had a family come in, passing through town. By the time they finished their lunch, they were on their way to Clingstone and to the bakery."

"That's a great idea."

She nodded. "I need to meet these people, talk to them."

"I can help."

"What?"

I grasped her hand. "I know these people. They're my neighbors. Some are friends. We all have a common goal. To make our livelihood with the land. I can introduce you. Smooth the way. Help with negotiations if needed." She opened her mouth, and I held up my finger. "Not that you can't negotiate, but I speak their language. I know what they need to hear."

She added ice cream to the bowls, looking thoughtful. I slipped a hand under her chin, lifting it. "Are you happy here, Quinn?"

"I love it here."

I cupped her cheek, and she turned, pressing a kiss to my palm. "Especially now," she added, her voice warm and soft.

"I want you happy. I want you to stay. Let me do this. Trust me enough to allow me to help."

"Okay."

Bending forward, I kissed her. Softly. I let her feel what I was feeling in that moment.

Then Abby ran in.

"Eww…again?" She scrambled up on her chair. "Can we have cobbler, or are you gonna keep kissing?"

I grinned against Quinn's mouth. "Both, I hope."

She pulled back, touching my bottom lip. "I'd say your chances were good, Farmer John."

"Excellent."

The days passed, somehow more quickly than before. My life seemed busier. Fuller. I realized it was because of the addition of two special people. Quinn and Abby were a constant now. I would drop by the restaurant for lunch. Go to Quinn's place in the evening, or she would come to the farmhouse. We saw each other most days. The ones we didn't seemed lonelier somehow. The more time we spent together, the closer we became. Quinn was more relaxed, the smile on her face now reaching her eyes. She was adjusting to her new life and seemed to love small-town living. Her friend Cathy came to see her, and I met her, seemingly getting her approval. We made plans to have dinner together with her and her husband one night. I knew the two women spoke on the phone often, and I was glad Quinn had a friend close by.

Abby resembled all the other kids her age. Running around, her feet dirty, hair mussed, and enjoying the freedom of summer and living a life without the boundaries her father had constantly placed on them. Her childish laughter rang out all the time. She was affectionate and open.

When I said so to Quinn, she had winked at me. "You're pretty affectionate and open, too."

She was right. Since the day she had kissed me at the restaurant, I'd had no issues pulling her in for a hug when I would see her. Kiss her tempting lips. Run my hand through her silky hair if I had the chance. She often laughed as I hauled her by the straps of the denim overalls she loved to wear to get her close enough to kiss, regardless of who was watching. At first, people seemed shocked, but now, they barely looked. It was the same with Abby. Anytime she saw me, I was greeted as if I'd been gone for months instead of a day, at times, even a matter of hours. They each made me feel special for different reasons.

And they made me smile more than I could recall doing my entire life.

My only complaint was the private time I got to spend with Quinn was rare. A few stolen hours after Abby fell asleep. The occasional late afternoon when Quinn was finished working and Abby was at a playdate. I couldn't get enough of being with Quinn. Touching her soft skin. Tasting her. Being buried inside her. Hearing her whispers, the low gasps of delight, the long moans, and the way she breathed out my name as she climaxed.

I was addicted.

But I knew I had to be patient. She was still finding her feet after her horrible marriage, and I grappled with trust at times. We knew we needed to allow time to heal and find our footing together in this relationship.

Some days were harder than others.

Summer heat began to build, and the fields needed extra attention. I was preparing the new land for a crop of fall rye. It was the right location on the property, and the produce had lots of usage. Quinn and Laura had worked the old garden, and I had rebuilt the fence around it to keep the animals out. Vegetables were growing, the plants once again thriving. My gramps would be thrilled to see it.

Watching Quinn work in the garden brought back so many memories. My grandmother tending the plants with Gramps beside her. My mom in the garden, helping. Me learning so much.

I wiped my forehead, peering up at the relentless sun. I turned the hose to my head, letting the cold water run over my scalp and face. It felt good. My shirt was soaked when I shook my head, the water scattering huge drops everywhere. The sun would dry it soon enough. It had been a solid week without a break in the high temperatures. Shading my eyes, I looked over the fields, worried about the water usage, the crops surviving, and work we needed to do to ensure it. I looked back at the garden beds, wishing a hose and a few moments of water worked the same on the large acreage, then shook my head at the thoughts.

If wishes were horses…was a saying my gramps would mutter when a neighbor wished for rain, for more sun, for whatever they needed at the moment. The truth was, all a farmer could do was keep working, tending, and praying. I knew that all too well.

Quinn and Abby were coming over tonight. We planned another evening by the watering hole, the water refreshing and helping to keep us cool. I had bought and built a gazebo, which offered us great shade. Bob and I had added some chairs and a nice table, and we made great use of it. Quinn was bringing a cold dinner we would eat in the shade, and I had a large jar of iced tea brewing in the sun, the way Mom had done for years. I added lemons, limes, and grapefruit, then sweetened it with honey the way she had taught me. Quinn loved it, exclaiming over the burst of citrus. Abby wasn't particularly interested, but she adored the watermelon lemonade I always had on hand for her.

I heard Quinn's SUV, turning and waving as she got out, helping Abby from the back. They headed over, Abby greeting me in her usual exuberant fashion. "Farmer John! You'll never guess what happened today!"

Quinn took the hose from me, and I brushed a kiss to her mouth before hunching in front of Abby. "What, Pumpkin?"

"I went down the slide too fast, and Joey was standing in front of it. I yelled, but he didn't move. I knocked him over, and he got mad and he pushed me. Bethy punched Joey and knocked his tooth right out!"

Bethy was Abby's "bestest" friend. She was wild. Rough and tough and didn't put up with any shit from anyone. And she loved Abby fiercely and was very protective. Hearing she'd punched a boy wasn't a shock, although I was sure her dad wasn't happy.

Since his wife had left him, he'd been trying to tame Bethy, but she was incredibly determined and outspoken.

"Did she apologize?" I asked, lifting my gaze to Quinn, who shook her head, trying not to laugh.

"Nope. He was madder than a hornet, but Bethy told him not to be such a whiny baby and to put the tooth under a pillow, and he'd get money. He was happy then."

I tried not to laugh. *"Not to be such a whiny baby."*

That little girl was something else. I feared for the man who fell for her one day.

And I felt equal parts worried and amused for her father, Jason.

"And Mommy and me made treats!"

I stood. "In this heat?"

Quinn laughed. "We did it at the restaurant in the cool."

"Is the house not cool?" I asked, worried.

"Not as nice as the restaurant. The air is cool, but not cold the past couple of days."

"I'll come look at it. Maybe it needs a top-up. You should have said something," I scolded gently.

"You're up to your eyeballs right now. We're fine."

"I'll look tomorrow."

"Thank you." She paused. "Laura and company coming tonight?"

"No. Cody has soccer practice and a team barbecue."

"So, I get you all to myself?" she asked with an exaggerated leer.

I bent close, brushing my lips over hers. "Every last inch."

"Yay, me."

I snickered. "Now, let's get our swim stuff and head to the water."

"We made submarine sandwiches and brought chips."

"Plus treats!" Abby added.

"Sounds great."

The water was refreshing, and I felt the lingering exhaustion the heat always brought lift off me. We ate the delicious sandwiches, and I smirked as I was offered a large square of Rice Krispies treat. I took the gooey treat eagerly. "Haven't had one of these in years." I bit down and chewed. "It tastes about a hundred times better than I remembered, and that was pretty damn tasty."

"Momma has a secret in…ingrad."

"Ingredient," Quinn corrected her.

"Yeah. Ingredient."

I took another bite, munching slowly. "It's very chewy."

"I add toffee to the marshmallows. Gives it more flavor."

"Great addition."

"I helped stir in the Krispies!" Abby informed me.

"I knew it had been stirred extra well," I said with a nod. "Great job, Pumpkin."

She beamed at me—one of her bright, sunny smiles. It took so little to make her happy. A kind word. A hug. A teddy bear.

"Can I swim again?"

"Yes, just make sure we can see you."

We watched as she launched herself into the water, floating on one of the toys we had.

"You are so good with her."

"It's easy to be good to her. She deserves it." I cleared my throat. "You both do."

Bending forward, Quinn pulled my mouth to hers, and I cupped the back of her head, groaning as her tongue stroked along mine. We kissed deeply, getting lost with each other until the splashing made us look up. Abby was observing us, obviously disgusted. Chuckling, I pressed one last kiss to Quinn's lips. "Eww," I murmured, using Abby's words from the other night. "Is that all you want to do to me? Kiss?"

Quinn lifted her eyebrows. "Not all."

My shorts suddenly felt tight, and I decided I needed to get in the water.

"I feel so used," I teased.

"Wait until later."

I was looking forward to that.

15

JOHN

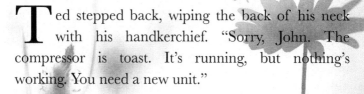

Ted stepped back, wiping the back of his neck with his handkerchief. "Sorry, John. The compressor is toast. It's running, but nothing's working. You need a new unit."

"Can you get me one?" I asked without hesitation. This morning, I had dropped by the Dill to get the keys from Quinn, and she looked exhausted.

"What's happened?" I asked. "Pumpkin have a bad night?" I knew she was prone to nightmares if upset.

"No. I think the air gave out. It was hot. Too hot to sleep, even with the windows open," Quinn replied. "We're both tired today."

"Why didn't you call?" I asked.

"No need for three of us to be exhausted. There was nothing you could do at one a.m."

I crowded her against the counter, my voice low. "I would have come and gotten you. Brought you to the farm where you could sleep comfortably." I traced the dark circles under her eyes. "I hate the fact that you didn't call."

She smiled wanly, and the kitchen door opened. I stepped back, holding out my hand for the keys. "I'll get it fixed."

"Thank you."

Ted shook his head. "Everything is back-ordered, John. I can't even get you a window unit to cool off a room right now. It's the same everywhere. This heat is killing everyone."

He tapped on his phone, flicking at the screen. "Two weeks. Minimum."

"Order it."

He nodded. "Will do. It's supposed to rain by the weekend. Although I'm not sure it will bring us much relief."

I ran a hand through my hair. "Can you check the other units? If they're going, I want them replaced as well."

Ted looked pleased. "You take good care of your tenants, John. I know my mom's is fine. I checked it last week. And we replaced one two years ago, but I'll make sure it's operating okay."

"You didn't send me a bill for your mom's place."

He laughed. "First, it's my mom. And second, you are always checking on her and doing things for her. The least I can do is check out her air conditioner and furnace. Both are good. But I'll check the other houses tomorrow. Today is pretty booked."

I shook his hand, and he left. I went inside, the temperature in the house even worse than outside. I grabbed a glass of water, leaning on the counter and sipping it as I looked around. Quinn had made the place homey. Comfortable. It was obvious she took care of the house well. But I couldn't let her stay here without air conditioning. The back door opened, and Laura walked in. I frowned. "What are you doing here?"

Laura smiled. "I went to have coffee, and Quinn told me what happened. As manager, I came to see if I could help."

I huffed out a laugh. "You mean to say you wanted to know what was going on."

She shrugged. "That too."

I sighed. "Ted's ordering a new unit."

"Oh, great."

I held up my hand, meeting her eyes. "Not great. Two weeks minimum."

She grimaced. "Ugh." She looked around. "I have a

couple extra fans. There must be some at the farm too. You only put in air a few years ago there."

"I can't let them stay here with no air."

She crossed her arms. "Two years ago, the Brightons' unit died. It was three days in the summer without air."

"It wasn't this hot." I sucked in a deep lungful of air. "And it wasn't Quinn and Pumpkin."

"So, what are you gonna do? Put them up in a hotel?"

I shook my head. "No. They're coming to the farm."

Ignoring her shocked look, I kept talking. "Can you let the tenants know we're doing an inspection to make sure everything is okay with their units? I want to get ahead of any problems."

She dug in her bag for her phone and list of tenants. "I know they'll appreciate it."

"Ted will let me know if there's a problem."

"Let's hope not. The farmhouse is going to get pretty crowded," she teased.

"One-time offer," I replied.

"One-house offer, you mean."

I smirked. She was right. The offer was always there now for Quinn and Abby. They were the exception.

I had a feeling they might always prove to be the exception.

"No, we're not," Quinn argued when I told her what Ted had said and my decision. "We'll be fine. We'll use the local pool at night. Borrow the fans from Laura. It's not like I haven't been in hot places before."

"No, you're packing a bag for each of you and coming to stay with me. It only makes sense."

Quinn leaned over the table. "John, we're tenants."

"You're more than that, and you know it. I can't let you and Pumpkin stay in that sweatbox. I swear it was ten degrees hotter inside than out. There isn't even a breeze. There isn't going to be. It's going to be hot and humid for another week at least. I have a big guest room. Pumpkin can swim anytime she wants. You'll be cool and able to sleep."

"She has things—"

I cut her off by holding up my hand. "I'll help you get her to her activities."

Quinn chewed the inside of her lip in indecision. I knew how hard it was for her to accept help.

"She has a sleepover tomorrow," she protested lamely.

I chuckled. "Perfect. I get her momma alone for the night."

She looked around. "People will talk."

I shrugged. "Let them. I don't care. All I care about is that you two will be safe and comfortable with me."

"Are you sure? Having us for dinner is one thing. Having us around all the time is another. I know you like your privacy."

I wasn't sure how to tell her I was tired of my privacy. Of being alone all the time. I wanted them with me. I was looking forward to having them there.

"I'm positive."

"I'll cook the meals."

"Even better."

"It's only until the unit is fixed. Maybe it'll arrive early."

"Maybe." I hadn't mentioned that Ted had called me and said it could be even longer. I kept that little bit of news to myself.

"I need to contrib—"

I stopped her with a shake of my head. "Don't even go there."

She sighed. "Okay. Thank you."

I got up to leave, bending over her in the corner booth. Other people were in the restaurant, but they were busy eating and talking. The town had gotten used to seeing us together, so it was no longer interesting. "Do you not know I would do anything to make sure you're okay, Quinn?" I murmured. "Always. You and Pumpkin are first for me now. You understand that?"

She blinked. "I'm trying to get used to it."

I lowered my head, capturing her mouth. I kissed her —far too long and passionately for public, but I didn't care. "Get used to it, then. It's not going to change." I straightened up. "I'll see you at the farm later."

She nodded, looking dazed. I headed to the door and out to my truck. I had things to prep before my girls arrived.

My work here was done.

QUINN

Later that afternoon, I picked up Abby from the sitter's. She looked tired and worn out. We headed toward the house, her steps dragging.

"How was camp, baby?"

"Too hot," she griped. "And Mrs. Grainger doesn't like cold air." She sighed, pushing her sweat-soaked hair off her forehead. "Can we go to the restaurant? It's cool there."

"Nope," I said with a grin. "We're going to Farmer John's. You can swim."

That made her smile.

"And you know what else?" I asked.

"What?"

"We're staying there until the air is fixed."

Her eyes widened. "Really? Like a sleepover?"

"Uh-huh. When we get home, we're gonna pack a little bag and go. You have to pick what you need, okay?"

"Enid and Fluffy have to come."

"Of course."

"Can I bring my toys?"

"Only a few."

"Okay," she agreed easily.

At the house, I was shocked by how hot it was inside. I was grateful for John's offer. And, if I was totally honest with myself, excited. The thought of seeing him more made me smile. The idea we'd have some alone time made the butterflies in my stomach dance. He had quickly become important to me. To both of us. Given my history, I should be wary, but I knew with John, it was different. He was different.

Abby raced to her room, and I followed, helping her pick some outfits and the essentials. Then I put a basket on the bed. "Only what fits in here for toys," I cautioned her.

"Not including Enid and Fluffy, right?" she bargained.

"Right."

In my room, I grabbed my suitcase and quickly packed. Overalls, T-shirts, a couple of nightshirts went into the bag. My toiletries and underwear. I hesitated, then added a couple of sundresses in case I needed them. I didn't pack a lot, knowing I could pop back and grab anything I needed.

I peeked in at Abby, who was still working on her toys —the decision of what came obviously very important.

In the kitchen, I grabbed anything from the fridge that might spoil while I was away and added a few things from the freezer and pantry. John might not let me contribute financially, but I could throw in a few groceries.

And cook him some great meals.

The man could eat. I knew he had to burn through calories every day with the physical labor he did. He needed to eat well to keep up his strength. I could at least make sure that happened. Plus, whatever other needs he had physically.

The thought of meeting those needs made me squeeze my thighs together. He excelled at that.

"Momma!" Abby's voice broke through my raunchy thoughts, and I turned to her.

"All ready?"

"Yep."

I followed her to her room, trying not to laugh at her toy basket. It was like a Jenga puzzle, each toy stuffed in well and rising high. I didn't have the heart to scold her or say no. Most of it was her stuffies, and I spied her little blanket she'd had since she was a baby in the bottom.

"Okay, baby. Let's get this in the car."

Not long after, we headed down the road toward John's. I knew he'd be in the fields working, and I planned on getting dinner ready for when he got home.

Maybe we could spend the evening at the swimming

hole. I was looking forward to a restful night's slumber in a cool house.

Plus, of course, whatever John planned on doing to help relax me. I had a feeling I would enjoy it.

At least twice.

If I was lucky, maybe three times.

John surprised me by being there when we arrived. He came out the door, smiling broadly, looking thrilled to see us. He swung Abby up into his arms, holding her as she told him about choosing her toys and how she'd made sure to pack extra swimsuits.

He was patient, listening to her as he carried her and the bags into the house, the effort seemingly nothing to him. I unpacked the food quickly, stashing it in the fridge and freezer, and deciding burgers on the grill tonight would be good.

He came in again, this time Abby beside him, still talking. "Is that right, Pumpkin?" he asked, looking serious. "That's how hot you were?"

She nodded. "My skin was melting, Farmer John. It was loose and felt funny. I was so glad when Momma arrived and the car was cool. I might have just been a puddle."

He frowned, throwing me a wink. "I would have tossed you in the freezer and fixed you right up."

She giggled, following him down the hall. I picked up my bag and traipsed behind them, enjoying listening to the conversation.

"How would you get me up from the ground?"

"A turkey baster," he said without missing a beat.

"What if you missed part of me?"

"I would have made sure to get every drop," he assured her.

"Okay." She sighed in apparent happiness, knowing that if she did indeed melt, Farmer John would save her.

"Now, since you were at melting level, I think we need to go have a swim. Make sure your insides are cool."

Her eyes widened with delight, and she opened her bag, her suit right on top. "I'll go change!"

She ran down the hall to the bathroom, closing the door with a little too much excitement. I looked at John. "Sorry you invited us yet?"

He crossed the room, yanking me to his chest. "Nope. Can't have my girls melting."

I chuckled. "You are so good with her. You listen and never talk down to her."

"She's smart. Funny. I love how she thinks. Why would I talk down to her?"

"Some people do."

"Like your ex?" he asked, narrowing his eyes. "He was an asshole, so I'm not surprised. I talk to her the way I've always talked to Cody. They're kids, not idiots. They have thoughts and ideas." He grinned. "Maybe not the most accurate ideas, but they deserve to be listened to, nonetheless."

Unable to stop myself, I pulled his head down and kissed him. He grunted in pleasure, tugging me closer and kissing me back. He tasted of coffee and mint. Smelled like grass, sunshine, and summer. I liked how he held me. Tight. Close. Preston always held himself back, as if worried about getting wrinkles in his clothing. He never hugged Abby unless we were out and he felt it was warranted for the moment, and even then, he was awkward. His wardrobe was always more important than expressing any feelings. Good ones, at least.

Abby raced down the hall, and we broke apart, both breathing heavily.

"What was that for?" John asked.

"Being you. Treating my daughter as if she matters."

He drifted his knuckles down my cheek. "You both matter, Quinn. Very much."

Then he bent and lifted Abby. "Let's go to the swimming hole!"

"You too, Momma?"

I nodded, fighting down the emotion John's simple words had evoked in me. My voice felt thick in my throat. "I'll just get my suit. I'll be down in a minute."

"What about you, Farmer John?" she asked.

"I got mine on already. I was prepared." He winked at me, his voice tender. "Take your time, darlin'. We'll be fine."

I heard their laughter down the hall and outside, and I drew in a long inhale. I was still getting used to this John. Open, sweet, funny.

But I was more than happy to get to know him a lot better.

Abby fell asleep, her hamburger half eaten, clutched in her hand. She had been talking and laughing, then got quiet for a minute, her head sinking to her chest.

John watched her, smiling tenderly. "I think we wore her out."

I reached over, plucking the burger from her hand and wiping her mouth. "Between melting all night and day, plus the swimming and the games you had her playing? I'm not surprised."

"What should we do?"

"Leave her for a few moments. She might wake up," I said, stroking her damp hair fondly. "If not, I'll carry her to bed, and she can have a good breakfast when she wakes up."

"Okay."

He finished his dinner, then sat back, observing her. "She looks so much like you."

"Except her eyes."

"Her dad's?" he guessed.

"Well, the color, yes. But hers are warm and expressive. Slightly lighter in color. His were very dark brown."

"She's like you in so many ways."

"We spent all our time together. I had to be Mom and Dad. He couldn't be bothered, and when he was around, he sucked the life out of whatever fun we had planned." I put my chin in my hand, looking at my daughter sleeping at the table, crumbs all around her and a streak of ketchup on her cheek I had missed.

"I don't know when he became so obsessed with money and reputation that he forgot how to laugh or live," I said quietly. "When he forgot he once loved me and wanted the same things I did. But it happened, and he wasn't the man I knew anymore. He wasn't the man I wanted to raise my daughter with. I loved her exactly the way she was. He wanted her to be a silent showpiece. A mini adult."

John slipped his hand under my chin, turning my face to his. "He was chasing the wrong dream. He got lost. He lost the greatest gifts he'd been given."

I smiled at his words.

"But I found you," he continued. "And my feet are firmly on the ground. I know what's important." He tightened his hand. "And I'm not letting go." He leaned close and kissed me. "I won't forget."

I touched his cheek, and we shared a long, intimate glance. His gaze was open. Warm. Telling me silently he had me.

"Let's take our girl to bed, Quinn. I think you're as exhausted as she is, and I am going to make sure you sleep well tonight."

"Promises, promises," I whispered.

"Ones I intend to keep."

16

JOHN

Abby didn't stir as we tucked her in. Quinn bent and kissed her forehead, leaving a small light on in case Abby woke up and was upset.

"Will you leave it on all night?"

"Yes. Even when I'm with her, she sometimes has nightmares in a strange place." Then she smiled, slipping her arm around my waist. "She's very happy here, though, so I'm hoping no bad dreams tonight. She isn't anxious. And neither am I. I always wondered if she picked up on my stress."

I drew her down the hall to my room. "I'm glad you're not stressed. But you're tired."

She glanced around my room in curiosity. She ran her hands over the twisted wood bed frame. "Did you make this?"

"Yeah."

"It's beautiful."

"Wood from the back lot that I cleared out," I explained. "I saw one on TV and thought how much I liked the look of it. I watched a bunch of YouTube videos and it took me a while, but I figured it out."

She took in the cream walls, the thick planked floors, and the simple furnishings. She was fascinated by the handmade rug on the floor, bending close to examine it.

"My grandmother made it. It's been in this house since it was built. Kinda faded now, but I still like it."

"It's amazing."

Her gaze strayed to the big armchair in the corner, taking in the table and pile of books on top. "I like to read," I murmured. "Relaxes me."

"Me too."

I indicated the door on the end wall. "I have something I think will relax you in there."

She met my eyes, hers dancing. I smirked. "Well, that too, darlin', but I thought you might like to soak a bit."

I led her through the large walk-in closet and to the bathroom. A huge, old-fashioned tub sat in the corner, the aged copper gleaming in the lights. She gasped in delight. "Oh my God—is that original?"

"Yep. Pulled it out of the old bathroom and had it replumbed when I added this new section to the house. It's deep and long, and I knew I wouldn't find anything like it. The copper holds the heat too."

She ran her fingers over the smooth metal. "It's so beautiful."

"You want a bath?"

"I would normally say yes, but I finally feel as if I'm not on fire anymore. Not sure I want the hot bath."

I chuckled. "Well, anytime you decide you do, it's here." I held out my hand. "Maybe I can figure out a different way to help you relax?" I asked, my voice low. "Something a little more…hands on?"

She let me pull her closer.

"I've been thinking about you all day, Quinn. Thinking about how you fell apart the other night so beautifully. How you looked. Tasted. Felt." I ran my mouth over her neck, sucking lightly on the skin. "Maybe we could revisit those memories?"

I felt her tremble. I pressed my lips to hers. "We can be quiet. Quick. Save long and loud for tomorrow."

"Just to take the edge off?" she whispered.

I burrowed one hand in her hair, ghosting up her rib cage with the other. "Yes. The edge."

"Or be quiet and long if she doesn't wake up?"

I laughed low in my chest. "Now you're talking."

Then I kissed her. I claimed her mouth, my tongue twisting with hers. She gripped my shoulders, whimpering in her throat. I lifted and carried her to my room, pushing my door almost shut, then laying her on the bed, following her down to the mattress. We kissed endlessly, our clothing disappearing until our bodies were flush. Every touch was magnified. Every taste an aphrodisiac. The feel of her skin on mine was silk. The scent of her surrounded us.

"John," she pleaded. "I want you."

"I want you too, baby. So bad. My cock is aching for you."

I gazed at her. "I want you to ride me, Quinn. I want to watch you."

Her eyes widened, doubts setting in. I shook my head. "Stay with me, baby. Right here in this moment. You are so beautiful. Remember that."

She pushed on my chest, and I rolled over so she could straddle me. She stopped for a moment, listening, always attuned to the other room. But it was silent, and she looked down at me, her cheeks flushed, eyes dazed. Her lips were swollen and wet, her hair in disarray from my hands.

I slipped my hand between us. "So wet, Quinn. You want this. You want me."

"Yes," she gasped, rolling her hips, taking my fingers deeper.

"You want my cock to fill you up? You want to ride me until you come? Until you drain me?" I murmured.

She became slicker, her arousal evident. I gripped her hips after I rolled on a condom. "Then do it, Quinn. Take me."

She grasped me, notching me to her entrance. Then she slowly, carefully, eased down on my length. I watched myself disappear into her inch by inch until we were flush.

I had never seen anything so erotic.

Then she began to move. Leisurely rolls of her hips, one hand on my chest, the other hand bunching her hair. I held her hips harder, guiding her. "Like that, my good girl. Just like that. Faster. Find your pleasure."

She began breathing faster. Moving quicker. She balanced both hands on my chest for a moment, then leaned back, grabbing my thighs, changing the angle and ramping up my pleasure.

Somehow being quiet made it incredibly intimate. Erotic. The sounds of our breathless whispers danced in the air.

"Yes. Oh God, yes."

"Move like that. Slide back. Fuck yes."

"You feel that, Quinn? You feel the way your pussy grips my cock?"

"Oh, that feels so good, John. I want more. Harder."

She moved quicker, the heat surrounding my cock indescribable. She made low, whimpering noises in her throat. Her hair tickled my legs. Her breasts swayed, and, unable to stop myself, I sat up, pulling her legs around my waist and seating myself deeper inside her. She gasped at the new angle and gripped my shoulders. I sucked one nipple in my mouth, then the other. I had never been so deep inside a woman, the sensations beginning to overwhelm me. I licked and bit the pink points until she was clawing at my skin, begging me. I moved her faster than ever, almost slamming her down on me. I hit her clit with every thrust, feeling her beginning to tighten around me.

"John," she moaned in a low whisper. "Oh God… Please. Please. Please."

"I'm coming, baby. I'm going to fucking come harder than I ever have before." I met her burning, desperate gaze. "And so are you."

Then I slammed my mouth over hers, and we climaxed. She screamed her release into my mouth, and I swallowed it down, my own roar silenced by our lips.

It felt as if the pleasure went on and on. As if we would never stop.

Until we did. Trembling, gasping, shaken, and exhausted. I wrapped my arms around her, pressing kisses to her head, lifting her face to mine and dropping small pecks of adoration all over her skin—cheeks, nose, chin, and eyes.

"Amazing," I breathed out. "You were amazing."

"*We* were amazing together," she replied.

I kissed her again, unable to stop myself. "Yeah, we were."

For a moment, neither of us moved, then I rolled her over, disposed of the condom, and grabbed my sweats, pulling them on.

Quinn sat up. "I should go sleep with Abby."

"Stay a bit." I handed her a T-shirt. "I want to hold you."

She slipped it over her head, and I crawled in beside her, pulling her into my arms. "Just for a little while," I added. "I like having you close."

She snuggled in, resting her head on my chest. "I like it too."

I shut my eyes with a contented sigh. Quinn laced our fingers together, and I lifted her hand to my mouth, kissing the soft skin. We didn't talk, each lost to our own thoughts. I was reeling from the way it felt to have her here in my bed. To know I would see her over my cup of coffee the next day. Hear her voice in the house. Even for a short time.

Or forever, a voice in my head whispered.

Somehow, that voice didn't bother me.

Something woke me, and I was instantly on alert. Quinn was beside me slumbering, her hand on my chest. I slid off the bed, listening, then heard it again. A quiet call coming down the hall.

"Momma?"

Abby's little voice was nervous. I hurried down the hall, going to the door and peeking my head in. She was sitting up in bed, looking around, clutching her doll.

"Hey, Pumpkin."

"Farmer John, I can't find my momma." She wiped her face, and my heart broke at the worry on it. She patted the bed. "She's supposed to be here!"

I walked in, sitting beside her and taking her hand. "You woke up and were scared?"

"Not scared. I like it here, but I can't find Momma." Her voice trembled. "Did she leave?"

Before I could answer, I heard Quinn's voice. "I was just in the kitchen getting water. You want some?" She padded in, holding out a glass. "Sorry, baby. I didn't hear you call. I was looking at the stars."

Abby took the glass, instantly relaxing when she saw Quinn.

"Stars?" she repeated.

Quinn gave her the glass, and Abby sipped from it. "Big stars?"

I exchanged a glance with Quinn, then stood. "You wanna come see, Pumpkin?"

She held out her arms, her worry gone, excitement in her voice. "Yes!"

I lifted her, and she nestled in my embrace, wrapping her arms around my neck. She talked to Quinn as we headed down the hall. "Why are the stars different here? How come you don't have a shirt on, Farmer John? Are you hot?"

"It's darker here," Quinn explained. "No pollution like in Toronto." Then under her breath, she muttered, "And yes, he is hot. Way too hot."

I tried not to grin.

"Oh."

Outside, I patted Abby's back. "Look up, Pumpkin."

She gazed upward in rapture. The sky was clear, and the stars shone brightly as if putting themselves on display for her.

"So pretty! Look at all the stars, Momma!"

"I know, baby."

"Can we look for a while?"

"Sure," I agreed easily and sat down on the porch, letting Abby settle on my knee. She peered at the sky, then gasped. "What was that?"

"A falling star," I explained.

"Ooh."

A moment later, she tilted her head toward me. "Farmer John, did the star fall to the bushes over there?" She pointed toward the boxwood.

I narrowed my eyes, looking, then chuckled. "No, Abby, those are fireflies."

"Fireflies?" she repeated. "What are those?"

"Little bugs. Their belly lights up as they fly."

"Why?"

"To help them find friends," I fibbed slightly. "It's their way of smiling."

"I've never seen one," Quinn said beside me.

"Me either," Abby agreed, leaning back into my chest.

"Big night for my girls. Bright stars, a shooting one, and fireflies." I pressed a kiss to Abby's head and grasped Quinn's hand, squeezing it.

"I like being your girl," Abby murmured.

That made me smile and I held her closer. "Maybe we can catch some fireflies one night, and you can see them up close. Then we can set them free."

"Okay," Abby whispered, relaxing even more into me. Quinn peeked over at her and nodded. She was falling back asleep. We stayed silent, and soon Abby was out, her breathing deep and even.

"I fell asleep," Quinn said. "Your mattress is too comfortable."

I kept my voice low. "My mattress or my chest?" I teased.

She hummed. "Same for both. I'm so glad you heard her."

"You did too, about thirty seconds after me. Don't beat yourself up over this, Quinn. She's fine. All she'll remember in the morning are the stars and the fireflies."

"Still, I better join her this time."

I understood. I carefully stood and carried Abby inside. Quinn lifted the covers, and I slid Abby in. Then I did the same for her. She hesitated. "Should I change?" she asked, fingering my shirt.

I shook my head. "It's a nightgown on you. Don't overthink. Now, in." I winked. "Besides, I'm too hot."

She blushed, making me snicker. "In," I said, indicating the bed.

I waited until she was settled, then bent and kissed her. "Sleep well, darlin'."

She smiled, cupping my cheek. "Probably not as well as when I was with you."

I winked. "Same."

I turned out the light and headed to my own bed. The sheets smelled like Quinn. Like us. I liked it, but I had to admit, it felt empty without her.

I was already looking forward to the next night. If Abby was able to spend the night at her friend's place, I'd get Quinn all to myself for the whole night.

I fell asleep with a smile on my face.

17

QUINN

The glass in my hand slipped, hitting the floor and shattering into hundreds of shards that scattered as far as my eyes could see. It took every ounce of restraint in me not to drop the other glass I was carrying and scream as it, too, exploded.

Instead, I drew in a deep inhale of oxygen, set down the other glass, and looked around the restaurant with a rueful smile. "Careful, everyone. I'll have this cleaned up in a jiffy."

The last few tables smiled and nodded, going back to their meals. The bell rang from the kitchen, and I was grateful the final order was ready. An unexpected, large group had shown up half an hour before closing, so we were going to be late. Still, it was good for business.

I went to the kitchen, grabbing the first tray, once again wishing I had help. Tammy had the day off, my other waitress, Jan, had called in sick, and I couldn't get hold of Chloe. So I was alone for the day. Then Kevin, the other staff member, called in sick as well. Normally, I could manage, but with the lingering heat, it seemed no one wanted to cook, and we had been extraordinarily busy all day. I heard the door open out front, and I rolled my eyes before going through the kitchen door. I had a feeling the day wouldn't be ending soon.

But as I went out front, I was greeted by John's confused smile as he sat at the counter. He rose to his feet, immediately reaching for the large tray. For a moment, I almost said no, and then I allowed him to take it. He followed me to the table and held it as I handed out plates.

"Right back with the rest," I promised.

"Can we get more water and coffee?" one customer asked.

"Of course."

I returned to the kitchen, loading the tray, hurrying back, and stopping in amazement. John was at the table, coffeepot and water pitcher in hand. He was pouring liquid, chatting with the customers, being charming. Friendly.

I had to blink and make sure I wasn't hallucinating.

"Ah, there she is," he said, meeting my gaze.

I crossed to the table, and once again, he held the tray as I gave out the rest of the plates.

"Anything else I can get you?"

"No," was the chorus I was pleased to hear. "John here got us ketchup and everything else while you were getting the food. We're good," one woman assured me. "I know we're late, so we'll eat up so you can close."

"Please take your time. It's not a problem," I lied.

They all began to eat, and I recalled I needed to clean up the glass. Except when I turned, I saw John by the booth, broom in hand. I approached him. "I'll finish that."

"Almost done." He looked around. "Where's your staff?"

I moved closer, dropping my voice. "Tammy has the day off. Jan called in sick, then about an hour later, the busboy, Kevin, did the same thing. I have a feeling they were being 'sick' together. I couldn't get hold of Chloe. And we've been crazy. Clint and I have been run off our feet."

"Tammy wouldn't have minded you calling her."

"She's at her in-laws for a birthday party. I didn't

want to take her from that. It's almost done. But I'm not going to get out of here on time."

He frowned.

I took in a deep breath. "Could you pick Abby up for me? Take her to the farm. I don't know what you can do when—"

He cut me off by laying a finger on my lips. "Yeah, I'll pick up Pumpkin and take her to the farm." He grinned widely. "She can come with me to finish the day. Check out the crops, ride on the tractor. She'll love it. We'll take her to the slumber party when you're done."

I worried my lip.

"Unless." He paused with a concerned tone. "Do you think she's okay for that?" he asked. "I was worried about that all morning. Wondering if being at the farm is enough of a change."

"She's slept at Mandy's before. She knows the other girls—and Bethy will be there. She's looking forward to it."

"Then we'll do that, and I'll take you to supper. If anything changes, we'll swing by and pick her up. No worries."

"Thank you," I breathed out.

Suddenly, he yanked me into his arms and, ignoring the fact that we had an audience, kissed me.

"Good girl," he whispered into my ear. "Asking me for help. I know how hard that is for you."

I couldn't help the flutter in my chest at his whispered praise.

I turned my head and pressed my mouth to his ear. "I like it when you call me good girl."

He stiffened, then chuckled low and satisfied in his chest. "Glad you do. I plan on calling you that tonight while your lips are wrapped around my cock. Then again when I take you hard and listen to you scream my name." His voice was like melted butter flowing over me, warm and sweet, the tone deep and sensuous. "We'll be alone tonight, darlin'. No holds barred."

I shivered, stared at him a moment, then I gripped his shirt and yanked him down to my level, kissing him as hard as he had done earlier, sliding my tongue over his.

He lifted his head with a lazy grin and touched my bottom lip, stroking it. "What was that for?"

"For being you. And all *that*—" I indicated the tables "—pouring water, being charming. Helping me."

He shook his head. "Your ex has a lot to answer for. That's what people in love do, Quinn. They help each other." With that word bomb, he dropped his head and kissed me again. "I'm going to get Clint to make me a sandwich and head out. I'll see you in a bit."

He walked away, and I stared after him.

Did he know what he'd just said?

Did he mean it?

I shook my head to clear it.

I'd have to find out later.

Right now, I had a restaurant to run.

JOHN

Abby looked up, squinting. I reached down on the floor and plunked a straw hat on her head. She giggled. "Now I'm a cowboy!"

"Not a cowboy. A farmer," I corrected. "A junior one."

"How come?"

"This is a farm, not a ranch. I have no livestock. No horses." I explained at her confused look. "I grow crops that feed people. It's important. I like being a farmer."

"You have cows. And you wear cowboy hats."

"I wear hats to keep the sun off my face like this." I tapped the brim of her too-big hat. "And if I were a cowboy, I'd ride a horse, and I'd have hundreds of cattle—not only a few dairy cows."

"Oh. Okay. I like being a farmer too, then. I really like horses too, but this tractor is cool. Can I steer again?"

"Yep." I placed her little hands on the big wheel, covering them with mine, and let her "steer" the tractor.

"Farmer John?"

"Yeah?"

"Are you Momma's serious boyfriend now?"

"Yes, I am."

"How come?"

"Because I think your momma is incredible. I think you are too. I like spending time with you."

"My dad didn't."

"Your dad is an idiot." Then I realized what I said and tried to backtrack. "Um, I mean, your dad…"

"…is an asshole," she finished. "That's what Momma says. But I can't say that to people." She glanced up. "But you're not people, right? You're Momma's. And mine. I like you, Farmer John. You're big and strong, and you wouldn't let me be gone."

"Gone?" I asked, slowing down the tractor. I had a feeling I was going to need to concentrate.

"I heard Dad tell Momma once, if she wasn't careful, one day I'd be gone, and she'd never find me. That made Momma cry. I kicked him, and he called me a brat and slammed the door so hard the wreath fell off, and the heart Momma had on it broke. That made her cry harder."

I shut my eyes before I spoke. No wonder Quinn was always on edge, and it explained Abby's trouble sleeping in new places. I tilted up Abby's chin. "Listen to me, Pumpkin, okay?"

She nodded.

"Nothing bad is ever going to happen to you. You will never be 'gone' from your momma. I won't let that happen. No one will ever take you away. You are safe here. It's my job to protect you now. Both of you."

"What is pro-protect?"

I turned her to look at the field. "You see that big covering in the corner? It's so hot there, I cover the plants to protect them from the sun so they're safe. They can grow and be the happiest plants because the sun can't hurt them."

"So, you're the cover?"

"Yes."

"What happens if you're not there?"

God, this kid was smart.

"I have little covers everywhere. If they thought you were in danger, they would let me know and protect you and your momma until I got there."

"Can I see them?"

"You can see them, but you won't know they're a cover. It's better that way."

"Like fairies?"

I chuckled. "Sort of."

She sighed. "I like that."

"So you don't have to worry anymore."

She turned, flinging her little arms around my neck. "I love you, Farmer John."

I hugged her back. "I love you too, Pumpkin."

She pulled back. "And Momma? Do you love her?"

18

JOHN

Quinn arrived later than planned, but early enough she had a chance to change before we took Abby to her slumber party.

Earlier, after she'd dropped her bombshell of a question, Abby had been distracted when the sprinklers came on suddenly, laughing as the cool water hit us. I cursed as I realized the timer must have malfunctioned, but it did stop me from having to answer her query.

Did I love her momma?

I was pretty certain that I did. It was fast, but it was real. And I knew it was forever.

But I really wanted to tell Quinn first before telling Abby. And I wanted to be sure Quinn was ready to hear it.

But every time I looked at her, every touch and every kiss only confirmed what I had been feeling. Quinn had somehow slipped into my heart without my realizing it, Abby following right behind her. They were a package deal, and I didn't plan on asking for a refund or any changes.

I liked it exactly how it came.

My girls.

We dropped Abby off, Quinn walking her in with her little knapsack and clutching Enid and Fluffy. I stayed in the truck, not wanting to overstep. Pumpkin had kissed me, flinging her arms around my neck. "Remember what I told you," I whispered.

She nodded, and I felt my stomach tighten a little as she left the truck. I had no idea how Quinn handled it.

Quinn came back, and I looked over at her. She looked worn and tired. "Do you want to just pick up a pizza, go home, and put our feet up? Have some wine, watch a movie, and be close, in case?"

"But you made plans."

I ran a finger down her cheek. "Darlin', as long as you're with me, then my plans are complete."

She sighed. "I'd love that."

I winked. "Done."

We picked up a pizza and headed to the farm. Quinn was quiet, staring out the window. I reached over and took her hand. "Something upsetting you?"

She turned her head with a rueful smile. "No. Just thinking about today."

"You planning on offering me a job? I have the need to tell you that pouring water and coffee are my only skills. I have a feeling carrying trays is beyond me."

She leaned her head back with a snicker. "You were awesome today. How is it you seem to know exactly what to do?"

"I don't," I admitted. "It's all guesses. And today, I happened to be in town to pick up some wood to rebuild the chicken coop ramp. I dropped by because I was hungry." I shrugged. "Didn't take many brains to figure out what was happening. You should have been closing, not serving a group of ten."

"But they were great. In fact, the mother told me her daughter wanted a different kind of wedding. A picnic. She asked if I catered because they all agreed the sandwiches and potato salad were the best they ever had. And that's what she wants on the menu. Sandwiches, salads, fresh fruit, cake. Lemonade and iced tea. They're getting married just themselves in the morning and want to do a country lunch after."

"Sounds like fun."

"I gave her my number, and she's going to call me next week. So, a late table would be worth it." She traced my arm as I pulled into the driveway. "But I was at my wit's end when you walked in. You made all the difference."

I parked the truck and leaned across the cab. "Glad I could help. Now, how about some pizza, a glass of wine, maybe a soak, and a movie? We can go to bed early." I waggled my eyebrows. "Seems to me I have a promise to keep."

"And if…" She trailed off.

"If Pumpkin needs picking up, I'll go. Just relax tonight, baby. Let me take the load."

She leaned close and kissed me, tangling her hand in my hair and pulling me close.

"Deal."

The pizza was delicious, tasting better somehow shared with Quinn on the sofa, a bottle of wine on the coffee table, napkins catching the messy sauce and dripping cheese. We talked about everything. The town. Growing up here. How Laura and Bob met. My parents.

We touched briefly on her past, but I knew it made her sad. She shared a few stories of spending time with her grandparents and liking it here.

"It was such a different place from the city," she explained. "I could run, play, be free. At home, I was more restricted. Once my parents died and my grandparents were in a home, the foster family I was with was right in the middle of the city." She smiled sadly. "I never got to see my grandparents again. They died close together less than a year after my parents."

I kissed her hand that was restlessly pulling on her denim-clad leg. "I'm sorry, baby. Were they good to you?"

She smiled. "They were nice people. I never felt as if I really belonged, though. I helped Joanna—the mother —a lot. She liked to cook, and I enjoyed it. It made me feel as if I wasn't taking more than I was given. He worked as a salesman, so he was gone a lot. But he was nice as well. Their kids were older than me and couldn't really be bothered one way or another." She lifted a shoulder. "I was lonely a lot. Which is probably why I fell so fast for Preston."

"Probably."

"Anyway, I missed coming out to the country. Life seemed simpler. Better. I wanted to give Abby the chance to experience living that way."

"And you are," I assured her. "I'll have her countrified in no time."

I got a real smile at my remark.

After we ate and she checked with Mandy's mom that Abby was doing okay, we watched a romantic comedy on the TV. It had been so long since I had done anything so domestic. More than once, I saw her roll her shoulders and stretch her legs as if they were sore, so when the movie was done, I headed to the bathroom and ran her a bath. I returned to the living room, trying not to laugh at the fact that she was dozing, curled up in the corner, her hand propped under her chin. She startled awake as I slid my arms under her and carried her down the hall.

"Put me down," she protested, even as she laid her head on my shoulder. "I can walk."

"I know you can, but right now, you don't have to."

In the bathroom, I set her on her feet, indicating the tub. "Soak. Relax."

"You joining me?"

I paused. I hadn't planned to, thinking she would enjoy a little quiet time, but the thought of her wet, naked, and relaxing against me was too much to resist.

"Absolutely."

In seconds, I was naked and slid into the tub, the sloped back fitting my frame well. I held out my hand and helped her step in, watching as she sank into the warm water with a satisfied sigh. For a moment, neither of us spoke.

"Sorry I don't have any bubble stuff."

She peeked at me over her shoulder. "Are you sure, John? You don't have a hidden stash and like to soak away your troubles at night in a sea of lavender-scented bubbles?" She winked. "You can tell me."

I let my head fall back in laughter. "You got me. But I prefer citrus."

"I'll remember that."

I cinched my arm around her waist, tucking her closer. I rested my chin on her head. "Never been in the tub. But my grandfather had this made for my grandmother years and years ago. He even helped. She loved to soak." I frowned. "At least, that was what he told me. Come to think of it, she was a pretty small woman. I fit in here with room to spare, which means he probably did too."

"When did she pass?"

"When I was a teenager. Gramps was never the same without her. I spent a lot of time with him."

"I'm sure he loved that."

I frowned, remembering how he slowly lost his will to live without her. The stories he shared about their life and how happy they had been. How much I still missed him.

Quinn nudged me, bringing me out of my sad thoughts.

"I bet they soaked together. Or something," Quinn said with a sly wink. "He probably helped her find the soap regularly. You know, so she could relax. I bet he looked hard."

I covered my eyes, grateful for her lightness. "Oh God, I don't want to think of them soaking together. Or the whole where's the soap thing. I doubt it was just to relax." Then I barked a laugh. "They were very affectionate. I bet they were pretty damned frisky, those two."

Quinn covered her mouth as she laughed. "This is quite roomy."

"It also explains why the old bathroom had a central drain in the floor. I thought Gramps was just ahead of his time."

"They probably flooded the room a few times," she said, sounding amused.

I pressed my fingers into my eyes. "Let's change the subject."

Quinn pushed forward, then spun and turned to me. She crooked her finger, indicating for me to come closer. I did, letting her wrap her legs around my waist. We were melded together, the warmth of the water around us. My cock pressed against her, and even with the water, I felt her desire. "Or we could make a flood of our own. Christen the tub."

She wrapped her arms around my neck, ghosting her mouth along the damp skin of my chest and shoulders. "Maybe I could ride you again." She tugged on my earlobe. "Maybe try reverse cowgirl."

I looked down at her, yearning coursing through my veins. "I didn't bring a condom."

"I'm on birth control. You can go bare. I feel safe with you."

"You are."

She waggled her eyebrows. "Bareback stallion-style."

I yanked her close, the movement causing the water to swell and splash over the edge.

"Yeehaw."

The next morning, we picked up Abby. Quinn looked

well rested and completely relaxed. I'd found the soap at least three times.

Then I had to dry her off in the bedroom. Really thoroughly.

I got her all wet again, though, so we had to have a shower.

And I found out my Quinn was really vocal when she wanted to be. We both enjoyed the freedom of no condoms. It was easily the most erotic sensation to be surrounded by her tight heat and feel everything so intensely. She seemed to like it, if the nail marks on my back and the love bite she left on my neck were any indications.

I returned the favor on her thighs and right over her heart.

I liked how she looked with my marks.

I wasn't sure when I had become such a possessive bastard.

Abby bolted out of the front door, running toward us, waving her arms in case we missed seeing her. "Hi, Momma! Hi, Farmer John!"

Then to my surprise and Quinn's shock, she headed straight to me, her arms outstretched. Bending, I picked her up, swinging her into my arms. She pressed her nose against mine. "Guess what?" she whispered excitedly.

"What?" I replied.

"I got scared last night, but I remembered what you said. And I told Mandy's mom, and she gave me some juice and talked to me till I wasn't scared anymore."

"What scared you?" I asked.

"It was darker than my room. But when I told her, she put a light on, and I was okay!" She dropped her voice. "Is she a cover too, John?"

I nodded. "Yep."

She nodded sagely. "I thought so."

Quinn watched us, a smile on her face. Abby turned to her, holding out her arms. "Hi!"

I handed her off, and Quinn dropped a bunch of little kisses on Abby's face, making her giggle.

"Momma!"

"I missed you. Did you have a good time?"

Abby nodded. "We watched a movie and had popcorn and chips. And we made the pizza and got to put on whatever we wanted!"

"Let me guess," I mused. "Hot peppers and anchovies?"

Abby wrinkled her nose. "No. Pepperoni and cheese with mushrooms and some bacon."

"That's my girl."

"Are we going to the farm?"

"Nope," I said. "I have a little surprise planned."

Quinn buckled Abby in the back, and I held open her door, helping her scramble into the seat. It amused me to watch. She was so petite compared to me. I bent and kissed her.

She cupped my face. "A surprise?"

I winked. "Yep."

We drove out of town for about thirty minutes and headed up a dirt road I knew well, pulling up to a large homestead. A group of men stood outside, and Abby stared at them as I swung her out of the back, perching her on my hip.

"Farmer John, are *those* cowboys?"

"Yep. This, Pumpkin, is a real ranch."

"With horses?"

"Yep. And you get to ride one today."

Her squeal was loud. "What about you and Momma?"

"Um, I think I'll just watch," Quinn said, sounding nervous.

I glanced her way. "Your choice, but you can ride with me if you want."

"Oh, um…"

"Please, Momma?"

"Okay. Maybe," she mumbled.

Laughing, I introduced her and Abby to my friend who owned the horse ranch. "Brent, this is Quinn. And this munchkin is Abby."

He greeted them, tipping his hat. He indicated the group with him. "My sons, Luke and Mike. My right hands, Joe and Taylor."

I shook their hands, and Abby and Quinn said hello. A woman came outside, wiping her hands on a dish towel. "And this is my wife, Sadie."

I leaned down and kissed her cheek. "Sadie. You're looking beautiful as always."

She waved me off. "Hush, you."

"We're gonna ride a horse," Abby told her.

"Yes, I heard. Then I have some cake and lemonade for after." She glanced at Quinn. "Are you joining them or coming inside?"

"Momma is coming," Abby said firmly.

Sadie laughed. "If you change your mind, the coffee is on. I hear you're quite the cook. We could swap some recipes. I plan on visiting your dill place next time I'm in town."

"You are always welcome," Quinn replied.

"Sadie here makes the best cakes I know. Didn't you used to sell them at the market?" I asked.

She nodded. "But when the stall closed down, I wasn't interested in what the new vendor was offering. I miss making them, strange as that sounds."

Quinn stepped forward. "I'm looking for local vendors for the restaurant. Maybe we could talk."

Sadie smiled. "I'd like that. You go for a short ride. Then we can chat."

"Okay."

Quinn looked decidedly more nervous as they brought out the horses. Abby had no fear, delighted at the small gelding they helped her up on. Quinn eyed the tall black stallion I swung myself onto. I held out my hand. "Come on, darlin'. It's perfectly safe."

"I think I'd rather go talk to Sadie."

"Ten minutes. Just ten minutes around the yard. If you're still nervous, we'll go out with Abby, and you can head inside."

She worried her lip, and I flicked my fingers. "Come up, baby."

"You don't have a saddle."

"Lots of room for you, then. Come on."

She gasped as Brent lifted her from behind, and I grasped her waist, sitting her in front of me. She grappled on my arms, her grip tight. "Relax," I breathed in her ear. "I have you."

I urged the horse forward, and we began a slow pace. Brent held the harness of Abby's horse, and she held the pommel, a wide grin on her face, not fearful at all. We trotted slowly around the yard, but Quinn never fully relaxed, her body pressed into me as close as she could get, her grip never easing.

"Not enjoying this?" I asked quietly.

"It's fine. Just not my thing."

I turned to Brent. "You go ahead. I'll catch up."

They moved out, a protective guard on either side of Abby. I slid off the horse and helped Quinn down. "Go have a chat with Sadie. I'll go with Pumpkin, and we'll be back soon."

"Sorry," she whispered.

"Hey." I lifted her chin. "Don't be sorry. You tried. Horses aren't your thing. No big deal. This was for

Abby, and as long as she has a good time, then all is great."

"I didn't want to disappoint you."

"You could never disappoint me, Quinn. I love you exactly the way you are. I don't want you to change."

We both froze as my words echoed around us.

"You love me?" she whispered.

I chuckled dryly. "Leave it to me to pick the least romantic spot to say it, but yeah, I love you, Quinn Harper. I don't know when or how, but somehow, I fell for you." I bent and kissed her. "Even when we argue, I love you. Nothing is gonna change that, and certainly not because you're not a horse fan. I kinda like that you're not big on cowboys."

"I'm a Farmer John fan," she said, her eyes glowing, her voice low.

"Then we're good."

"And I love you too. I don't know how either, but I do, John. I love you so much."

I swept her into my arms and kissed her. There was nothing left to say.

19

QUINN

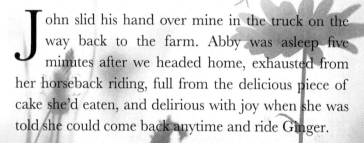

John slid his hand over mine in the truck on the way back to the farm. Abby was asleep five minutes after we headed home, exhausted from her horseback riding, full from the delicious piece of cake she'd eaten, and delirious with joy when she was told she could come back anytime and ride Ginger.

"She's so pretty, Momma! And she ate an apple from my hand and kissed it! She likes me."

"Pumpkin had a good day," he mused.

"She did."

"I was thinking of buying Ginger for her. We could stable her at the ranch."

I gaped at him. "Let's not get ahead of ourselves, John. She loves it today, maybe not in a week or a month."

He pursed his lips. "She's a steady little thing," he said, looking thoughtful. "I think she'll keep wanting to go. And when she shows she can do it, we can move the horse to the farm, and she can care for it there and ride her anytime she wants."

I felt a flutter in my chest at his words. I still hadn't gotten over the fact that he'd told me he loved me. Now, he was talking future plans.

Talk about steady.

When I had joined Sadie, she'd filled up a coffee mug and slid it my way. "Nice to see John look happy." She winked. "That's rare."

I had laughed and taken a sip of my coffee.

"He's crazy about you and the little one," she mused.

"Why would you say that?" I asked, curious.

"The way he looks at you. Both of you, actually. Protective. Loving. His father used to look at his mother the same way. They were a wonderful couple."

I felt myself blush. "He is pretty awesome. The gruffness is to keep people away."

She nodded, looking thoughtful. "I've known him a long time. He became gruffer the past few years." She eyed me knowingly. "And I'm sure you know why." She tutted under her breath. "That woman was awful. He deserves so much better." She patted my hand. "And I think he's found it."

"I think I'm pretty lucky."

She eyed me over the rim of her cup. "I'm a pretty good judge of character. I'd say he's lucked out as well." She smiled at my red cheeks. "Now, tell me about your plans."

"John," I admonished gently. "We don't have to rush things."

"Not trying to rush anything." He shrugged. "Those are my thoughts, so I'm letting you know. No worries." He glanced at me. "I'm a straight shooter, Quinn. I love you. I said it and I meant it. I plan on moving forward with you and Pumpkin. You want that too, right?"

"Yes. But—"

He shook his head. "But nothing. We'll do what we want, when we want. I have never let society or anyone dictate my life to me, and frankly, you let someone else dictate to you long enough. You tell me what you want, I'll tell you what I want, and we'll figure things out. And what I want is a life with you and Abby in it."

The words were out before I could stop them.

"Do you really want children?"

He flashed me a wide grin. "With you? Absolutely. I want to make a few of *her* all over again." He indicated Abby sleeping in the back seat. "Get to be there with you to go through everything. Hold them as a baby. Watch them take their first step." He paused. "As long as you want more."

"Yes, I do."

"Then we agree."

"Um, not like tomorrow."

He laughed, lifting my hand to his mouth. "Good. I want to spoil you for a while. Let you get to know me and all my bad habits, then decide if you want to risk my DNA mixing with yours."

"I love mixing our DNA."

He winked as he pulled into the driveway. "Later, darlin'. I promise you lots of DNA later."

I squeezed his hand. "Okay."

Abby woke up as we parked, and we headed down to the watering hole, the coolness refreshing on our skin. She splashed and played, John tossing her into the deeper water, staying close to make sure she was safe. I watched how natural they were together. How in tune he was with her, and I could only imagine him if I was pregnant. The protectiveness I saw in him would be multiplied.

Not that I minded.

I lounged in the shallower end, laughing when they joined me, Abby's hair wet and John looking like a drowned rat. I had heard lots of splashing.

"Having a good day, baby?" I asked Abby.

"The best."

"Good."

She grabbed one of the toys, floating on it, looking thoughtful. She turned to me. "Momma, what are we doing next weekend?"

"Um, nothing."

"But it's your birthday. We always do something fun on your birthday."

John's head snapped my way, and I felt his stare. He came closer, looming over me in the water.

"It's your birthday next week?"

I waved him off. "Yes."

"Why didn't you say anything?"

"It's not a big deal," I protested.

"It is, Momma. We have a special day!"

"What is it you do for your birthday?" John asked.

Abby grabbed his arm. "Last year, we went to a salon, and I had a pedicure! Then we went to a movie. After, we had McDonald's. It was so fun!"

John tilted his head. "I bet it was."

"The year before, we went to a pizza place. They thought it was my birthday, so I got a piece of cake, which made me laugh. But I shared it with Momma, and I got to play in the ball room. She watched and said it was the best day ever."

John nodded, his eyes on me. "I see."

I smiled. "I'll think of something, Abby."

John shook his head. "Oh no. I think this year, I get to make the birthday plans."

I opened my mouth to protest, but he shook his head again in warning.

"My plans," he murmured, lowering his head. "And you should have told me."

"I don't make a big deal of it," I whispered. "I make the day fun for her."

"Well, things have changed. Both my girls will be having fun. And I won't hear any arguments, Quinn." He met my eyes. "Right?"

He was serious, his gaze steady. I swallowed hard.

"Right."

He kissed me, hard and fast.

"Good girl."

JOHN

Later that evening, I sat on the porch. Quinn came outside to join me, sitting in the other rocker. I sipped a coffee, and she had a bottle of water.

"Abby asleep?"

"As soon as her head hit the pillow. She sleeps so well these days."

"She feels safe."

She glanced at me. "Yes, she does. She told me what you said to her—about covers, John. I think it gave her something she needed to hear." She paused, her voice filled with wonder. "You know exactly how to make her feel safe and looked after. Important."

"She is all those things. So are you."

She smiled. "I know."

"Do you?"

"Of course. You show me all the time."

"Why didn't you tell me it was your birthday next week, Quinn? Were you really going to let it pass without letting me know?"

She looked sad, crossing her legs and rocking in silence for a moment. "I didn't purposely not tell you. It's just…" She trailed off.

"Just what?"

"My birthday was never a big thing after I went into foster care. Preston took me out for a fancy dinner when we were dating to celebrate, but once we were married, I was lucky if he remembered it. I only ever did something on it with Abby because she loved her birthday so much. I tried to make hers special, and when she asked about mine, I made up things that seemed like they were for me…" She shrugged.

"But they were for her."

"It hasn't been a big deal for a long time."

"It is to me. I think the day you were born should be celebrated. So, we are going back to making it a big deal. And we can do it in a way that still includes Pumpkin."

"That would be nice," she said, but she still looked sad.

I reached out and took her hand. "Hey, I'm not mad. I want to understand, though. And I want you to realize things are different now. You matter. What you think matters. How you feel matters. And I want you happy."

She cupped my face. "Oh, John, I *am* happy."

"Then let me celebrate the day with you."

"What did you have in mind?"

"What about a trip into the city? You said you've never been to the aquarium. I thought it was awesome, and I think Pumpkin would love it. I checked, and there's an afternoon cruise on the harbor. We'll do lunch at the CN Tower because the view is spectacular, and you've never been. You and I will do a late dinner together—the hotel has childcare, so Abby will be looked after and everyone gets what they want. Pumpkin is included, I get to celebrate you, and you get to enjoy the day. Laura is planning a family dinner on Sunday, so they get a chance to celebrate you as well."

I watched as tears filled her eyes. "When did you plan all this?" she said with a sob.

"This afternoon, while you and Abby worked in the garden. I called Laura, and between us, we figured it out fast. She helped me make the reservations." I held out my hand. "Come here, darlin'."

She let me pull her to my lap, and I wrapped her in my arms. "Why the tears?" I asked, wanting to understand.

She was quiet for a moment, and I allowed her to gather her thoughts.

"I've been invisible for so long," she whispered. "I haven't been important enough to bother planning something to celebrate my birthday since my parents died."

"You're important to me." I tilted up her chin. "You've become the focus for me. I want to celebrate the day. Celebrate you."

"Okay," she sniffed. "That would be lovely."

"Quinn." I waited until she met my eyes. I wiped away the tears on her cheeks. "Those days are behind you. You aren't going to be alone anymore. You and Abby are mine. My family will be yours. *We* will be a family. Hopefully, a growing one. You will never be unimportant again. I swear that to you."

She buried her face into my neck and wept. I held her tight, letting her tears soak into my shirt. She needed to cry it out. I remembered my mom saying that to my dad about Laura when he'd expressed his worries about her teenage emotions.

"Girls and women sometimes need to cry, dear. It's our way of letting out the fear and worries we keep inside so we can start fresh."

So I rocked us, letting Quinn cry out her fear and worry. And when she was ready, we'd start again fresh. I was determined to show her a life where she was important. I'd love her until she forgot about the past and the loneliness and only knew how deeply she was adored.

QUINN

All week, I was excited about the upcoming weekend. The last birthday I had celebrated, there had been cake, balloons, and presents, and my parents and grandparents. I had been a child and filled with excitement and delight. At the foster home, if they remembered, I was wished a good day, and on occasion, Joanne made a dessert I liked, but it wasn't often. Still, I felt obligated not to complain. And Preston ignored the day after the one dinner. Once, he stopped as he was leaving the house and looked at me.

"It's your birthday," he said with a frown.

I shook my head. "Last week."

"Oh."

I waited, hoping he would smile and say he'd make it up tonight, but he simply shrugged. "Don't forget to pick up my dry cleaning." Then he walked out.

Once Abby was old enough, I'd do fun things with her to celebrate. It was more for her than me, although sharing the day with her made me feel a little better.

But this year, John had taken over the planning, and I had to admit, I was looking forward to the day.

On Thursday, I stopped by the house to pick up a dress I had that would be suitable for dinner on the weekend. Inside, I was startled to feel the cool air greet me as I walked in. I went back outside, surprised to see a new air conditioning unit installed and running quietly.

I returned to the kitchen, perplexed. John hadn't mentioned the air was fixed. I hesitated, then took the dress I'd picked, plus a couple more outfits for Abby, then headed back to the farm. I saw the tractor in the fields and knew John would have Abby with him. She adored him, and he felt the same way back. I never imagined the man I'd traded barbed words with would ever be the sweet, protective lover I had fallen for so quickly.

In the kitchen, I chuckled at the pile of fresh-shucked corn that sat on the counter. John had mentioned he had a small section of corn ready to pick, so I assumed corn was on the menu tonight.

I knew there was cold chicken, so I put together a nice Caesar salad and decided to grill the corn and serve it with a compound butter. I got it ready, smiling as I heard the heavy footsteps on the porch outside.

The door swung open, and John and Abby came in, both looking hot, tired, and happy. I couldn't recall my daughter ever looking this happy. She glowed these days. "Hey, you two."

I was greeted with kisses and hellos, which I was happy to get, although they both smelled a little ripe.

"How're the crops?" I asked.

"Desperate for the rain that is supposed to come tonight," he replied, sitting down heavily and accepting the cold water I offered him. "I hope it rains as long and steady as they're predicting. We all need it."

"Were you, ah, working in the barn?"

He chuckled. "I was fertilizing earlier. I know I smell. I'll go shower."

Abby wrinkled her nose. "Manure, Momma. It helps the plants grow."

"Ah."

She nodded sagely. "Cow shit."

I had to swallow back my laugh. "Abby," I choked out.

"It is. Farmer John told me."

I met his amused eyes. "I was explaining it to her. How we reuse things other people would think are useless."

"Like cow shit," Abby said again. "It's better than pig shit because of cooties."

"E. coli," John corrected gently.

"That's what I said. Farmers make shit useful. It's good for the envir-envir… What is it, Farmer John?"

"Environment."

"Yes. Most people don't know that, Momma. But us farmers do."

I tamped down my chuckle and put on a straight face. "You call it manure, Abby. Not cow shit. That can be considered a bad word."

She scratched her nose. "Like asshole? Farmer John says some of the men in town are assholes and about as useless as pig shit. I mean, manure." She turned to John. "Is it still manure if it's pig shit, Farmer John?"

He was looking everywhere but at me, and I knew he was trying not to laugh. "Yes, it is."

She looked thoughtful. "So, some shit is better than others."

"That pretty much sums it up." John made a funny noise, stood, and cleared his throat. "I'm going to go take that shower."

And like a coward, he hurried down the hall. He barely got the bedroom door shut before I heard him start to laugh.

With a sigh, I sat down and explained to my daughter why some of the things Farmer John muttered needed to be kept at home.

"You don't use those words in public with strangers and other people, Abby."

She looked at me as if I were crazy. "I know that, Momma. But we're at home. And Farmer John says we can be ourselves at home and say what's on our mind."

I rubbed the back of my neck. "Well, your mind needs to think polite words, young lady."

She stood. "Farmers have different ways of thinking, Momma. I'm a farmer now. You better become one too so you get it."

And she walked down the hall.

For a moment, I was in shock. Then I went outside, around the corner, and I laughed.

I decided Farmer John needed a good talking-to.

Dinner was interesting. John looked everywhere but at me, trying not to laugh. I'd given him a fast dressing-down while he'd stood in the shower, the water sluicing over his shoulders and back. He'd continued to soap himself up, trying to look abashed but failing.

"It's kinda funny, Quinn. No one would take offense here."

"Not the point."

"Jesus, she is smart. She said it best. Some shit is better than others."

"Stop laughing."

"You wanna come in here and let me apologize?"

"No!"

He grinned. "I'd make you forget about manure."

I turned and headed back to the kitchen.

But not before reaching in and turning off the hot water.

His yelp of surprise gave me more than a little satisfaction.

Abby prattled on about her day. "Bethy taught me how to karate chop someone," she said. "Take down a bully."

John looked impressed. "You need to show me later, Pumpkin."

"We don't karate chop people, Abby," I said, trying to stay patient.

"What if they karate chop me first?"

"We use our words."

"Well…" John began.

"*Our words*," I stressed.

"Yes, your momma is right. Words first, but if they come at you, then you can defend yourself."

I sighed and changed the subject. "I stopped by the house earlier to get a dress."

John's fork stopped halfway to his mouth. He looked guilty. "Oh."

"The air is fixed?"

"Yeah. Ted found a unit. Put it in today."

"So we can head home after the weekend." I looked at Abby. "You must miss your room?"

She shrugged.

"But you picked the paint," I reminded her.

"I like it here."

"You liked the house too. With the swing, remember?"

"I guess."

She pushed away her plate. "Momma, may I be excused?"

"You're finished?"

"I'm not hungry anymore."

"Of course."

She headed down the hall, and I glanced at John. He'd stopped eating as well. "The house was awfully cool for only having that unit put in today, John."

He balled up his napkin. "Okay, it went in on Tuesday."

"Why didn't you say anything?"

"Because I like having you here. I like coming home, knowing you and Pumpkin will be here. Hearing you laugh. Playing with her. Sleeping beside you. I didn't want you to go yet." He indicated the direction Abby had headed in. "I don't think she wants to go either."

"We have to go back eventually."

He met my eyes. "Why?" he challenged.

"That's our new home."

"This can be your new home. Here. With me. I can paint her room pink. Move her swing. She likes it here. She feels safe. You like it here."

"Of course I like it here, but that's not the point."

"What is?"

"John," I said gently. "We're so new. You really want to rush into moving in together?"

His eyes never left mine. "Yes."

"Wow," I mouthed, shocked. "I thought we were going to take it slow and make sure we're ready."

"I am ready. Move in with me."

I opened my mouth to tell him no, but the words didn't come out. My common sense told me to say it. Convince him it was too soon and too much.

But my heart was rejoicing. The thought of living here all the time made me want to yell the word yes and launch myself at him. Stay here—with him. Be part of his family. Have this be my home.

"I need some time."

He stood and bent over me. "Fine. You think about it. But think about this, Quinn Harper. You're mine and I'm yours. We're a done deal. Why should we wait to be happy? I think we both deserve that now. And one more thing to consider." His mouth covered mine, and he kissed me with a hunger that left me no doubt as to his thoughts. "You and me in our bed every night. Waking up with each other. Being parents for Abby. The whole package."

Then he walked away.

Later, I sat on the porch, watching John and Abby wrestle. She showed him her karate chop, and he decided she needed a few more pointers. I had given up trying to stop him. He was on his knees so he was closer to her height, and they were play fighting.

"Gimme your best shot, Pumpkin," he encouraged her.

She raced forward, hands clenched into fists, and drove them into his arm. He looked down, nonplussed.

"That's a punch, not a karate chop."

She frowned. "Oh yeah. Bethy showed me punches too." She rocked back on her heels, flexing her fingers like a martial arts expert, made a whoop noise, and karate-chopped him on the same arm.

"Pretty good," he said. "Now, let's put some weight behind it."

The next twenty minutes, he was patience personified, showing her how to throw a punch properly and use the momentum of motion for her karate chop.

"Let's try again. Run toward me and let me have it."

"Karate chop or punch?"

"Surprise me."

She moved backward, swinging her arms. Then she rushed toward him, delivering a single punch to his chest, and he went down like a felled tree. She jumped on him, laughing, and he lifted her high, making her squeal and yelp in delight. I had a feeling her punch had barely registered, but he wanted her to have some confidence.

A memory stirred, one I had long forgotten. My grandpa and me on the front lawn, doing much the same thing. Him pretending I was stronger than I was and fake-diving to the grass, then tickling me and lifting me, letting me be the victor. I recalled the laughter and the joy of the simple moment, and suddenly, I realized that was what had been missing in our lives.

Even though I had walked away from Preston, I still expected Abby to be a little lady. With John, she was simply being a child. Preston had been against roughhousing or any tomboyish activities. I was less strict, but I didn't know how to be that person with her. I had forgotten.

John was showing her. Letting her be Abby. It didn't make her less of a girl. It simply added to her experience.

And he was right—if she was bullied, she should be able to stand up for herself. He wasn't teaching her to fight. He was teaching her to defend. Be her own hero. And he was doing it in a fun, nonconfrontational way.

I got up and walked over to them. They looked up, expecting me to scold or tell them to stop. Neither of them expected me to drop to my knees and waggle my fingers at John. "Why don't you pick on someone your own size, buddy."

A delighted smile crossed his face. Abby clapped her hands. "Show him, Momma!"

John lunged, and I rolled out of the way. I tackled him from behind, and the game was on.

Loud peals of laughter followed as the three of us scuffled, wrestled, and practiced karate chops and punches as the evening waned away.

These were memories I hoped Abby would never forget.

20

JOHN

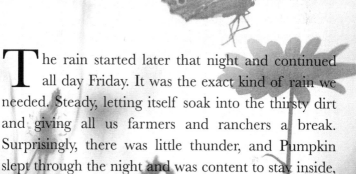

The rain started later that night and continued all day Friday. It was the exact kind of rain we needed. Steady, letting itself soak into the thirsty dirt and giving all us farmers and ranchers a break. Surprisingly, there was little thunder, and Pumpkin slept through the night and was content to stay inside, coloring and playing with her dolls.

"I think you wore her out last night," Quinn murmured. "All the wrestling."

I grinned at her over my cup of coffee, rubbing my chest. "Some more practice and she'll be good. Her last punch landed okay. Not a lot of power, but that seems better for her than the karate chop."

She smiled with me, and I winked. "What about her momma? I wear her out too with all the mattress-wrestling that happened?"

Quinn's cheeks colored, and I chuckled. I loved the fact that after sucking my cock and begging me to fuck her hard, she could blush if I mentioned sex.

It was endearing to me.

And I meant what I had said last night. I wanted her to stay. I wanted my girls in my house. It made it a home again. I wanted to sleep with Quinn every night and wake up to her every day. I wanted to be in trouble for teaching Abby about shit and laughing about it together later like we did last night.

I wanted forever.

Now I just had to convince her she wanted it too.

"You ready to leave tomorrow morning early? We have ten a.m. admission to the aquarium."

"Yes." She sat back, running a hand through her hair. "It feels odd not to be at work. I feel lazy."

I chuckled. "Perks of being the boss. Trust me, the place will not be busy. When it rains like this, everyone stays home and uses the downtime. I guarantee you Tammy will close up early."

"I told her to do that if it was quiet."

"Besides, consider it the start of your birthday weekend."

She rolled her eyes. "I go from no birthday to a whole weekend? Not sure I can cope with that." She got up from the table, heading to the sink. "One day is fine."

I caught her around the waist, pulling her to my lap and kissing her soundly. "Weekend, darlin'. It'll take me all weekend to celebrate you."

She met my eyes, hers soft and warm, the green vibrant this morning. "I love you," she whispered.

I kissed her again. "Love you right back."

We were in the truck bright and early, all of us anxious to start our adventure. I had woken Quinn up early, making love to her, then giving her the first gift of many to come. The simple gold chain with an infinity symbol on it glinted on her neck when she turned to me with a wide smile as she buckled her seat belt. She wore a pretty sundress in blues and greens with a headband keeping her long hair off her face and highlighting her eyes. I loved it when she wore her hair down. She still had on sneakers, but they were blue and lacy, and she looked lovely. Abby wore a pink dress and matching sneakers, and her hair was done in a French braid with pink ribbons to match her outfit woven into it.

I wore a button-down and dark jeans. I'd realized my sneakers were a mess, so I pulled on a pair of cowboy boots Laura had given me. They were comfortable, and I knew how much walking we'd be doing, so I was okay with it. I knew Abby and Quinn would get a kick out of my choice of footwear. I'd save my less-than-comfortable dress shoes for dinner later. I brought my only suit, and I knew Quinn had a dress for the evening. I was looking forward to having her all to myself later. Abby was excited at the prospect of the movie night with other kids and the crafts listed. All in all, it was a day we were all looking forward to.

Abby asked a multitude of questions on the way into Toronto. I knew her world there had been very sequestered and not happy. I told her as many stories as I could about the places we were going, wanting to keep up her excitement.

We arrived at the aquarium on time, and with the crowds around us, I lifted her onto my hip, holding her tight until we got inside. I kept my other hand wrapped around Quinn's.

As we approached the doors, I looked down at Abby's excited face. "Ready, Pumpkin?"

"Ready!"

"Let's go, then."

I leaned over the table, smiling at Abby. "What was your favorite part?"

"The dolphins," she replied immediately, holding up the pink heart-covered stuffed dolphin I had bought her at the gift shop. "And the sharks," she added. "The colored jelly ones. All the fishes!"

"So, all of it?" I asked.

"Yes!"

She'd been in awe. Turning her head constantly so as not to miss anything. Asking questions, staring at the overhead tunnel, laughing in delight at the antics of some of the fish and the dolphins. Quinn had been entranced as well, and I was glad I had been before since I had a hard time tearing my gaze away from their enjoyment.

On the elevator ride up the CN Tower, Abby had been nervous, but she relaxed when I picked her up, and she nestled into my side. In the restaurant, she had looked around, mesmerized by the view from the table, but unimpressed otherwise. The lunch was really more for Quinn. Luckily, they had a decent kids menu, and Abby was enthusiastic about the chicken fingers option.

Quinn sipped her wine, staring at the vast expanse laid out before us. We had selected the charcuterie appetizer, and I ordered the steak, while Quinn chose the blackened chicken. Abby snacked on a few bits from our appetizer and was now busy chatting up her new stuffie, telling her all about Enid and Fluffy.

I leaned over to Quinn. "Having a good day so far, darlin'?"

"Amazing," she replied.

"We'll check in to the hotel after, then walk over to the boat."

There was a small ruckus at a table across the restaurant, a man's condescending tone reaching my ears. I shared a grimace with Quinn. "Someone's not happy."

"I used to hate going to restaurants with Preston. He always complained about something. Demanded to speak to the manager and get some sort of compensation. I found it embarrassing."

"Some people are like that."

Our food arrived, and I rubbed my hands together. "Ignore them and let's enjoy our meal."

Quinn nodded. "Sounds good."

We ate and talked about the aquarium and the upcoming boat trip. Abby, as usual, was droll and clever, making me laugh. I had preordered dessert, and Quinn's eyes were round, her cheeks flushed with embarrassment as a small cake was placed on the table and the staff sang happy birthday to her. We ate the rich dessert, somehow finishing the whole thing, even as we protested about being too full. It was a great lunch, and I was almost giddy with how well the day was going.

That feeling came to a complete and abrupt halt as we headed to the elevator, Abby between us. The lobby area was empty except for one couple waiting already, their backs to us. There was something recognizable about the woman, but I couldn't place her. Something about her height and the tilt of her head seemed familiar. The man beside her spoke, and I recognized the timbre of his voice as the complainer in the restaurant. Quinn gasped quietly when he talked, stepping back. I looked at her, concerned, as the couple turned and the identity of the woman became clear to me. As did the man to Quinn.

Quinn's voice was horrified as she spoke.

"Preston?"

I glared at the woman clinging to his arm, my voice a low snarl.

"Moira."

QUINN

For a moment, we all stared. I felt as if I were trapped in some farce, and I waited for someone to yell *Gotcha!* But it didn't happen. Abby pressed into my side, staring up at her father, her grip on my hand tightening. I felt John's anger, and I stared at the woman standing beside my ex.

There was no denying she was beautiful. Her hair and makeup perfect. Her clothes probably worth more than my rent for a month. But if you looked closely, you saw the coldness in her eyes, the pinched look on her face, and the boredom of her expression.

Preston had changed since I'd seen him last. Though he'd always been tall and lanky, now his shoulders were more rounded than before, his posture not as stiff as it used to be. He'd grown a beard, and his hair, something he'd fussed and preened over, had thinned some and was now more gray than dark. He wore glasses, another new addition, and the frown lines around his mouth and forehead were deep. He looked discontented and haughty.

A look that only grew when he saw me and Abby.

"Quinn," he said in a mocking tone. "What a surprise to see you." His gaze flickered to Abby. "And Abigail."

"Abby," she responded.

He lifted his eyebrows. "Typical," he muttered.

John made a low noise in his throat, and Preston cast a look at him, slowly taking in his stance. His gaze lingered on his boots. He chuckled, the sound dry and nasty. "Dating a cowboy now, Quinn? How…quaint."

Abby dropped my hand, folding her arms over her chest the way John did when he was upset.

"He isn't a cowboy. He's a *farmer*. That's important."

Preston ignored her the way he always did.

"I heard you moved to some hick town, Quinn. No doubt you fit in well with the locals. Having a big day in the city, are we?" His pitch was condescending, bordering on snide.

His fiancée snickered, covering her mouth, the large diamond on her hand ridiculous and ostentatious.

John took a step closer. "Watch your tone."

Preston smirked. "Or what? You'll plant me?"

"We're here celebrating Quinn's birthday," John replied, ignoring his jibe. "Not that you'd understand how that works."

A dull red soaked Preston's cheeks. He hated being called out for what a lousy husband he had been. It was John's turn to smirk.

"And I'm taking *my girls* for a fun afternoon. Shocking, no one did that when they lived here. As if someone couldn't be bothered to look after them. Treat them the way they should be treated."

"That's enough," I said quietly. I had no desire to stand here and trade insults with my ex and his cold partner. "Let's go."

Preston glared at me. "Maybe I'd like to spend some time with Abigail. We could catch up."

I knew he was saying that to upset me. He had zero interest in "catching up" with his daughter.

"Over my dead body," I hissed at the same time John cursed. But what was the most shocking was Abby's reaction.

"No," she said loudly. "I don't like you, and you're not my dad. Farmer John is the best daddy ever. He's nice to me. He makes Momma smile. You were mean."

Preston glared. "Be silent," he demanded. At John's huff, he glared. "Back off, cowboy. This doesn't concern you."

"No!" she said louder. "Farmer John is the best. You —you are just an *asshole*!"

"What did you say?" he snapped.

"*Asshole!*" she repeated, once again crossing her arms. "*Useless as pig shit.*"

I gasped, John smothered a laugh, and then Preston's face turned darker.

"This is how you raised her?" he snarled. "To be a mouthy, classless little brat?"

His hand flexed, and for a terrible moment, I thought he would attempt to strike her. I grabbed at Abby to push her behind me and John moved to block him, but Abby was faster than anyone. She ducked under my arm, lunged forward, her hands raised—and nailed Preston right in the nuts.

He gasped, dropping to his knees.

"You're pig shit!" she repeated. *"Full of cooties!"*

Shocked, I stepped back, watching my daughter yelling at her father, calling him *pig shit*. Taking him down with a punch to the junk. Berating him for calling John a cowboy.

"Farmers!" she insisted. "We are *farmers!"*

I had no idea how to react. I met John's eyes. It was a mistake. He was amused. Highly amused. He lifted a shoulder. "She's right. We *are* farmers." He leaned closer, his voice low. "I guess punching *is* the way to go for her. Highly effective at that height."

And suddenly, I was laughing. Uncontrollably.

John joined me, and our mirth was unforgivable. Outrageous. Undignified.

John bent and scooped Abby away from Preston, who looked shell-shocked. John handed her to me. "That's good, Pumpkin. I think you got your point across."

Abby buried her face into my chest. I stroked up and down her back in comforting passes. He stared down with disgust at Preston, who glared back, furious, embarrassed, and ready to fight.

"I will sue."

John rolled his eyes. "What will you tell the court? That your six-year-old you abandoned without a thought took you down and let the world know you're not even good enough to be cow shit?" He bent, his voice low and filled with rage, and he gripped Preston's shoulder. "Let's get one thing very clear. They are my concern because *they are mine.* And I protect what's mine. You come near either of them, you cause one bit of trouble, and I will make sure your nuts are never in working order again. You understand me?"

Preston grunted, the bully backing down when challenged. "Get away from me," he said, shaking off John's hold and rising to his feet. "I tripped, obviously."

John shook his head. "Whatever lets you sleep at night." He turned to me, taking Abby. "I think our girl has said all that needs to be said. Unless you have something more you want to run by Abby?" he asked Preston, an evil grin on his face.

Preston seemed to shrink away. "We're done here."

John nodded. "I thought so."

Ignoring the few people now watching us, I pressed the elevator button, relieved when it opened, and we stepped in. John stopped the doors closing, indicating Moira, who had done nothing except stare and look aghast and somewhat disgusted. "And good luck with that one. I'd watch my bank accounts if I were you."

Preston turned to Moira. "What does he mean by that? How do you know the cowboy?"

"*Farmer!*" we all yelled in unison as the doors shut.

Then I was laughing again.

And it felt good.

John carried Abby to the car, holding my hand tight. Once we got there, he stroked Abby's back. "You okay, Pumpkin?"

She pulled her tearstained face from his neck. "I don't like him."

"I know. Me either." He whispered something to her that made her smile. I was fairly certain he was agreeing with her about the asshole part.

She looked at me. "I used my words, Momma. They didn't work."

"I know, baby," I assured her, still stunned.

"Am I in trouble? Because I said shit and I punched him? Do we have to go home so I can have a time-out?"

I looked at her and John. I recalled the look on Preston's face as Abby junk-punched him. The lingering thought that his last memory of his daughter would be that a six-year-old brought him to his knees and informed him he was less than cow shit. He was pig shit. Full of cooties. It was certainly a memory I would never forget.

"Baby, you couldn't have given Momma a better present."

JOHN

At the hotel, I checked us in, and we headed up to the suite. Abby had fallen asleep on the short drive over, and I carried her with her head on my chest. No doubt, she was exhausted from the emotional scene that had occurred. The front desk staff had been charmed by her, whispering about the sweet little thing I was holding.

It was all I could do not to tell them she had just taken down a grown man who insulted us.

In the suite, I laid her on the bed, and Quinn hovered over her, pulling off her shoes and brushing her hair off her forehead. "What time do we have to be at the boat?"

"Not until four. It's a short walk, so let her rest." Unable to stop myself, I chuckled. "Champ deserves it."

"John," she hissed, and I pulled her from the room and to the sofa.

"Quinn," I said, amusement still coursing through me. "Don't go backward and get upset." I hung my head, my shoulders shaking with mirth. "That was epic."

"My daughter just assaulted her father."

"Who was making some fast hand gestures indicating his ire. I think she felt threatened."

"You saw that too?"

I nodded. "Your little girl just let her anger out and showed the man who walked away that she was stronger than he will ever be. I know getting hit in the nuts isn't fun, but she is *six*. He outweighs her by over a hundred pounds and has fully developed muscles. I highly doubt she was strong enough to do much damage. He's a fucking wuss."

"She was pretty mad," she agreed. "The whole cowboy thing was upsetting her, now that she's a farmer and all."

I nodded. "Defending our people."

A snort escaped her lips, and she tried to look serious. "Do you think I need to get her more therapy for some residual anger issues?"

I started to laugh so hard, I fell back on the sofa.

Quinn glared at me. "That was a serious question."

I sat up, wiping my eyes. "I'm a simple man, Quinn. You know this. I don't quite understand the whole therapy thing, but if you think she needs it, we'll get her more. Or if she wants to talk, we'll listen. If she has anger issues, I'll get out my old punching bag and hang it in the shed, and she can punch the shit out of it." I huffed out a long breath of air. "I think she was mad. Upset. Caught off guard. That's gotta be hard for a kid. And she remembered our bully talk. It was an extraordinary set of emotions and, frankly, a fucked-up encounter. We all reacted, but she reacted the fastest. It doesn't mean she's suddenly going to be punching everything that upsets her."

"If she does?"

"Then we'll deal with it." I met her eyes. "Together."

She rubbed her head, and I let her process for a minute. She fell back on the cushion, covering her eyes.

"I need to talk to her."

"I agree." I nudged her. "She called me the best daddy."

"I heard."

"I think we should talk to her together."

She peered at me from between her fingers. "In that talk, you are not going to use the words epic, asshole, or pig shit."

"What about cooties?"

"John," she warned.

"Can I high-five her for the nut-punch? I really hope there is security cam footage or someone caught that on their phone. I would blow it up into a motivational poster. David and Goliath sort of thing."

Quinn bit her lip, trying to stay serious and not laugh.

"Junk-punch—not just for adults."

She lost it, slapping her hand over her mouth and laughing.

I wanted her to laugh. To see the twisted beauty behind the event. We would be adults and talk to Abby, but right now, Quinn needed this release.

"Someday you will remind her of this, and she'll be horrified," I said, pulling her close and kissing her.

"I hope it becomes a distant memory to her."

"I hope she never forgets it," I insisted. "And she isn't being punished, right?"

"No," she sighed. "The whole thing was punishment enough."

"Good."

I tugged her head to my chest. "Relax a bit, darlin'. I think we all need a bit of recovery time."

She snuggled closer. "Yeah."

I woke up to Abby's smiling face looking at me. "Hey, Pumpkin."

"Hi."

I glanced at my watch. "We have to leave in about twenty minutes. Where's Momma?"

"Right here."

I looked over my shoulder to see Quinn in the corner. She was watching us quietly.

"Everything okay?"

Abby leaned closer. "Momma and me talked while you were sleeping."

I was glad they'd had some time to discuss what had happened earlier. "I see."

"I'm not in trouble."

"No, you're not."

"But I won't punch people."

"Good plan."

She dropped her voice, covering her mouth, as if telling me a secret. "You're not supposed to teach me no more bad words, Farmer John. Momma says I'm like a parrot."

I had to contain my smile. My bad words had been used perfectly today, but I knew I couldn't say that. "Momma is right," I said seriously. "No more punching or bad words."

Then Abby smiled. "But Momma is going to put me in real karate classes!"

"Well, that's a good idea."

"I think another good idea is we get ready to go," Quinn stated.

Abby scrambled off my chest. "I'll get my shoes!"

I sat up. "She seems fine."

"You were right, I think. She is fine. We talked, and I'm leaving it alone now."

I stood and pulled her off the sofa. "Good. Can we forget about him and go back to the birthday celebrations?"

She smiled at me. "Yes." She patted my chest. "Are you okay? I mean seeing, ah, *her?*"

"The only thing I thought when I saw her was how grateful I was not to be him. And once I knew who he was, I decided he deserved whatever she did. I hope she drains him dry."

"Even after your warning?"

I chuckled. "She'll sweet-talk her way out of it. But at least I would have made her sweat a little. And he deserves what he gets. Between the epic junk-punch from Abby and the one coming from her eventually, he's in for a world of pain."

Amusement danced in her eyes. "Couldn't happen to a better asshole."

I nodded. "Cooties."

She giggled. "Full of 'em."

"How they met, I have no idea, but she has obviously recreated herself again. And this time, he was the idiot that fell for it. I think they're both going to suffer."

"She's pretty," Quinn offered. "He likes that."

I shook my head. "She's hard and fake. She might have the outside package he is looking for, but inside, she is a cesspool of greed and selfishness." I trailed my fingers down her cheek. "You're real. Beautiful—inside and out. There is nothing fake about you. And I love you."

She kissed my finger resting on her cheek. "I love you."

I winked. "Now, let's go make some more great memories, darlin'."

"I'd love to."

The rest of the afternoon was a quandary. There were moments of laughter. Lots of smiles from Abby, but Quinn's seemed forced at times. I caught her more than once looking upset, but when she would see me studying her, she forced a smile to her face and a lighthearted tone to her voice. Internally, I cursed running into her ex. He had spoiled what should have been a perfect day for Quinn. Secretly, I wished I'd had the chance for one good punch myself.

Instead, I was living vicariously through a child who had the satisfaction of throwing said punch.

The boat ride was wonderful, the sun and breeze refreshing, the views of the city spectacular. Quinn finally relaxed and seemed to be enjoying herself. We took turns pointing out different things to Abby, who, as usual, asked lots of questions.

I got her a gooey funnel cake, and we sat at a table, watching the city as it went by.

"Wow," Quinn said in amazement, looking at the horizon. "Too many buildings."

I chuckled. "Too many people."

Quinn leaned her head on my shoulder. "I like our view better."

I pressed a kiss to her head. "Me too."

When the boat docked, we took a walk, then headed back to the hotel. Abby wanted a bubble bath, so Quinn filled the tub, adding bubbles, and left her happily singing a made-up song about her boat ride.

I watched Quinn for a few moments, curious. Something had been off since she and Abby had talked. I couldn't put my finger on it, but Quinn was too quiet. I needed to know what had upset her. Did it have to do with the talk with Abby, or was the earlier incident still playing on repeat in her head?

She stood by the window, staring out at the skyline. I wrapped my arms around her. "Miss the city?"

"No."

I buried my head into her neck. "Miss our little Richton?"

"Yes."

"We'll go home in the morning."

"Good."

"You okay?"

"I'm good," she replied too quickly.

"Quinn…"

She turned in my arms, looking troubled.

"What is it?"

"Would you be upset if we didn't go to dinner? If we stayed here and ordered in room service?"

"If you wanted to go home, I'd be okay with it. Whatever you want to do, Quinn. Today is your day. Whatever makes you happy."

"You do. You make me happy."

"Then why do you look so sad?"

She hesitated, and I took her hands. "I thought we were past you hiding from me."

She looked down at our joined fingers. A tear splashing on my skin made me hold them tighter.

"Tell me."

Her voice shook when she spoke. "She thought he was going to hit me. That's why she punched him."

I had thought the same thing from the furious look on his face, which was why I had started to block him. But hearing Quinn's words, my rage was instant. "I thought you said he didn't hit you."

"He hit me once, years ago. But he knew the words hurt more, so he used those as his weapon of choice. But he liked to grab me, scream in my face. I learned to tell when he was about to. His hand would flex, the way it did just before—" She swallowed and met my eyes. "I didn't know she saw that too."

"That bastard."

"How can a small child notice something like that?" she whispered. "She never said anything to me until today."

"She is incredibly smart," I assured her. "She gets that from you."

"I should have left sooner."

"You left when you could. Stop beating yourself up. Stop questioning your choices. You can't change them." I lifted her chin to mine. "She is fine, Quinn. Thriving, even. And today hasn't set her back. Listen to her singing, telling her dolphin friend her stories. She's happy. She's safe. I know it sounds stupid, but junk-punching him was probably therapeutic for her. She knows she doesn't have to fear him. And she has us. We'll make sure she stays okay. We'll find a therapist if you think she needs one. But, baby…stop, please." I shook my head. "I wish I had kicked his ass. I still want to. He needs a good beatdown. Especially with this new information." I huffed. "If I had known that, I would have taken him out. Put him in the hospital. I'm still tempted."

"I don't want you near him. I need you. I need you with me."

I folded her into my arms. "I am. Now, I need you with me. In the present."

"Ask me what I miss the most about Richton."

"What?" I asked fondly.

"The farm." Her lips trembled. "I don't want to go back to my house tomorrow. I want to stay with you."

Delight flooded me. I cupped her face. "Quinn, baby. Are you sure?"

"I don't want to wait to be happy. You make me happy. You make Abby happy. You're right. You're it for us too, John. We both love you."

I tugged her close. "Then we'll have our own party in the room with our girl and order in whatever you want. Tomorrow, we'll go home, and you'll stay." I drew in a long breath. "On one condition."

Easing back, she frowned, tensing. "Which is?"

"You stay—as my wife."

Her eyes widened.

"Marry me, Quinn. Let me adopt Abby. Let's be a real family. Let's make sure nothing and nobody can take her away from us."

She was speechless.

"Quinn and Abby Elliott has a nice ring to it, don't you think?"

She flung her arms around my neck.

"Yes!"

QUINN

Richton came into view, and I sighed happily. I glanced at John, who met my eyes and winked. He knew how much I wanted to come home. Last night, I had no doubt that if I said I wanted to leave right then, he would have calmly checked us out, driven us home, and never uttered another word about it.

But we stayed. Ordered room service. Watched a silly movie with Abby. He understood without saying a word that I simply couldn't leave her last night. Not with what had happened and what she had confessed to me.

"I would hear yelling and look, Momma," she whispered. "He was always mad. And his hand pumped. I saw it yesterday and thought he was gonna hurt you. I had to stop him."

My heart had cracked at her words.

I had cupped her face and pressed kisses everywhere. "You are so brave, baby. But it's my job to look after you. Your job is to be a little girl."

She had smiled up at me. "Now that Farmer John found us, I can. He protects us."

John was right. She was smart beyond her years. "Yes, he does."

"He loves us. He told me."

"He told me too."

I smiled in happiness as we turned up the driveway to the farm. Home. I was home.

I had felt more at home here in the past days than I had ever felt anywhere in my adult life. John was home. With him, I was safe. Loved.

And I was never leaving this place, or him, again.

John stopped the truck and turned off the ignition. "We're home, family."

Family.

I finally had it.

"So, I asked Quinn to marry me," John said casually as we sipped coffee after dinner at Laura's dining room table. She had gone all out, making a delicious meal and having a birthday cake for me. There had even been a few gifts. Thoughtful, heartfelt ones I would use and love.

I watched Laura carefully for her reaction, worried she would feel it was too soon and we were rushing into it. Instead, there was only joy as she sprang from her chair and hugged me, then John. Bob followed suit and shook John's hand. He glanced at his wife with a wink.

"You called it, honey."

John looked at his sister. "Called what?"

Laura laughed as Bob explained. "She came home from the town hall meeting and told me you'd be married before the fall. Probably sooner. And she was right."

John gaped at her. "You thought that back then?"

Laura shook her head. "You couldn't vote against her. You were trying so hard to hold on to your curmudgeonly ways, but they were already slipping. I saw the way you looked at her when you thought no one was looking." She threw a wink at me. "And how you glanced at him, Quinn. I could feel the connection between you."

"So you threw out the swing suggestion?" John questioned her.

"Once you let it slip you had kissed her, I knew I had to push you along." She shrugged. "It worked, didn't it?"

John laughed. "Yeah, it did."

"When and where is the wedding happening?" Then she frowned. "Why aren't you wearing a ring? Was it too big? How did you propose? After dinner? Tell me all the details."

We exchanged glances.

"Ah, it was a spur-of-the-moment thing. No ring. Nothing fancy."

Laura frowned. "You don't have a ring?"

"I don't need one. I have his heart. I'd like a band once we get married, but we need to work out all the details."

"What aren't you telling us?"

John looked over his shoulder. The kids were playing outside on the trampoline. He drew in a deep breath and told them the story of my birthday. They listened, their eyes growing round as John told them about what Abby had done. I added what she had told me and how I needed to stay close. John finished with him asking me to stay and be his wife.

For a moment, they said nothing, then Bob snickered.

"Dammit, I wish I had seen the takedown."

Laura grinned. "I bet it was epic."

John grinned. "It was."

We shared a laugh, especially when John reenacted the way Preston fell. "What a wimp. She's a quarter of his size. I'm surprised she even found anything to hit."

I chuckled. Compared to John, Preston was certainly lacking in size and knowledge. Sex with him had never been great, but he'd always told me it was my fault. I knew differently now.

Laura shook her head. "How is it she is so like you with no shared DNA?"

"What?"

"Don't you remember?"

"Remember what?"

She leaned forward, happy to tell her story.

"You were about ten. It was later in the day, and Dad was in the storeroom. Mom had a difficult customer who was arguing with her at the counter. You didn't like how aggressive he was being, and suddenly, you grabbed a rake from the display beside the register and told this guy to back off and leave your mother alone. I ran and got Dad. He calmed everyone down, and the customer apologized and left. You were so upset, and Dad took you out back. I thought you were going to get punished for yelling at a customer, so I followed to ask him not to. But Dad hugged you and said he was proud of you for protecting your mom. After he closed the store, he took us all out for ice cream, but you got a triple scoop." She tilted her head. "You don't recall that?"

John huffed out a laugh. "Now that you reminded me, I do." He grinned at me. "I guess Pumpkin *is* like me. Must be the farmer gene that has kicked in."

We all laughed.

He winked. "I'm good with that."

I leaned forward and kissed him. "Me too."

Laura clapped her hands. "Okay, let's discuss this wedding."

I sat on the porch, the cool of the evening welcome. Abby was asleep in her bed, tucked up with Enid, Fluffy, and Flipper, the new dolphin. She was happy and content. She had had no nightmares last night, and not once had she mentioned her father or what had happened. John was right. It was a moment, and she wasn't dwelling on it, so neither was I.

We had chatted about various options with Laura. All we really knew was we wanted to be married soon and it would be small.

I liked the idea of being married here, in the backyard, with his family and a few friends. The only people I would invite would be Cathy and her family and my staff.

John seemed fine with it, although Laura had a place she wanted me to see. I agreed because she seemed so excited to show it to me.

John came out, sitting next to me, but first dropping a kiss to my mouth. "Hey."

I cupped his face, bringing it back to mine. "Hi."

He rocked for a moment. "You don't have to go look at this place with Laura. She's just excited."

"I don't mind."

"She says it's pretty." He bumped my foot with his. "I want you to have pretty."

I reached out my hand, and we laced our fingers together.

"The fireflies are busy tonight," I observed.

"They are." He looked thoughtful. "Maybe we could get married in the evening and have little blinking lights."

"That would be nice," I agreed.

He sighed. "Laura gave me shit."

"About?"

"I told you I loved you in a totally unromantic way. I asked you to marry me without getting on one knee, no ring, and no flowery promises. She says I botched it up."

I shook my head. "I disagree. I love that you told me for no reason. And your proposal was said with love. I don't need the flowery promises. I need you. Your heart. Your love."

"You have it. All of it. But if you like the pretty place, I want you to have that too, okay?"

I smiled. "Okay."

He stood, holding out his hand. "Let's go to bed, darlin'. I've got some fireflies lighting up my pants I want to show you."

I let him pull me from the chair. "I can hardly wait to see."

It was Friday before we made it to see the venue. The week had been busy at the restaurant and on the farm. Still, John found time to load up my furniture and bring it out to the farm, rebuilding the bedroom set in the other guest room for Abby, who was beyond thrilled we were staying. I wasn't sure her feet were touching the ground yet. Every day, John would appear at the restaurant and follow me to the house to help me pack up a few boxes to add to our ever-growing invasion of the farmhouse. But his smile never left his face, and last night, I had looked around, amazed how quickly emptying the place had happened. It helped when your landlord owned the house, had family and staff with trucks, and was determined not to give you a chance to change your mind.

Not that I would. He made me too happy.

Laura picked me up since John told me he was really busy with some farm work that afternoon. Abby had a playdate with Bethy, which gave me the time to go and see the venue.

"If you like it, I'll come with you next week," he assured me.

We pulled up to a nice homestead, the lawn green and the flowers swaying in the breeze. Laura followed the driveway around back and parked in the large lot, pointing at a small building. "That's it. It's called Shades of Light."

"How did you find out about it?"

"It's my client's. She is getting ready to open it, and she agreed to let you see it and use it as a practice run if you want it."

Her phone rang, and she looked at the screen. "I have to take this. Go in and see what you think."

I approached the building, taking in the old wood, the charming elements of the flowers and shrubs, the small rock fountains bubbling away in the sun, and the soaring pitch to the roof. Inside, I stood in awe. The ceiling was all glass, as was the back wall that looked out onto a wooded area. There were fairy lights everywhere. Beams and huge wooden pillars that soared twenty feet in the air. More flowers and decorations. The room was set up with tables and would easily hold sixty people or more, depending on how it was arranged. I could already see it at night with candles flickering, the stars overhead, and music playing. Laura had told me there was another building that housed a kitchen for catering and a space for the wedding parties to prepare in. I walked to the back, staring at the trees. I could see they, too, were strung with lights, and I could only imagine them at night.

The building was beyond pretty, and suddenly, I desperately wanted to marry John here. I knew he'd love it as well.

I heard the door open behind me and footsteps.

"I wish John could see this," I said.

"Well then, darlin', you got your wish."

I spun with a gasp. Behind me stood John, holding Abby, who was beaming. She clutched flowers in her arms. "Hi, Momma."

I had to swallow before speaking. "Hi, baby." I walked toward them. "What are you doing here?"

John nudged Abby with a wink. "Being romantic."

She giggled and extended the flowers my way. I took them, kissing her cheek, then rising on my toes to kiss John.

He smiled. "Beautiful."

"It is."

"I meant you."

"Oh."

He pulled out a chair, indicating I should sit. Once I did, he set Abby on my knee.

"I like this place."

"I think it would be magical at night."

He nodded, then dropped to a knee in front of me. "Let's add a little day magic, okay?"

"John," I whispered, feeling breathless. "What are you—"

"Shh, Momma. He needs to talk," Abby said, tapping her lips.

I nodded, the tears already forming in my eyes even as I grinned at her bossiness.

"I'm not good at romantic gestures, Quinn, but I'd like to spend the rest of my life getting better at them. With you."

He took in a deep breath. "You agreed to marry me as part of a demand, and I think your life has had too many demands already. I want it to be because you want to. I want you to marry me as much as I want to marry you. We both want a simple life, but I think, together, we'll make it extraordinary."

He reached out and took my hand and Abby's. "I want to marry you both. Make you my family. We can start with the three of us and build from there. Make a life together. With me, your hearts are safe. You are safe. You belong with me."

He dug in his pocket and pulled out a flat box, handing it to Abby. She opened it and squealed at the pretty gold pumpkin with tiny emeralds for eyes. "You stole my heart with your smile, Pumpkin. Can I marry your momma and be your daddy for the rest of my life?"

She launched herself at him, hugging him hard. "Yes!"

He sat her on his knee. "Your turn, Quinn. I know you said you didn't need a ring, but I wanted you to have one." He indicated the bow on the flowers. "That one is very special to me. I never thought I would meet a woman amazing enough to give it to, but you have proven me wrong."

I looked down, picking up the ribbon, where a ring sat. The wide gold band was dotted with emeralds and diamonds. Small, twinkly gems that glimmered in the light. "This belonged to my gram. My gramps gave it to me with the farm and told me one day I'd find the right person to share both with. And darlin'— that's you." He swallowed and paused. "Will you marry me, Quinn? Make my life complete? Let me belong to you?"

Unable to speak, I nodded. He took the ring off the ribbon, sliding it on my finger.

He smiled. "Perfect. Just like you."

Then he kissed me.

And I knew my life had changed forever.

John was right. Together, we would be extraordinary.

It was as simple as that.

EPILOGUE

A LITTLE OVER A YEAR LATER

QUINN

I wandered the venue, straightening a fork, retucking a napkin, making sure everything was perfect. It didn't matter how often I walked this floor, looked at the wall of glass, or watched as a couple took their first spin on the dance floor as husband and wife, this room took my breath away.

I sat on a chair, recalling my wedding to John, a year ago today. We had been married late in the evening, as the sun dipped below the horizon and darkness kissed the sky. The fairy lights glowing around us, the flickering of the candles, and the scent of the flowers were things I would always recall about that day.

John wore a suit, looking handsome and sexy, a single rose pinned on his lapel. Abby wore a sparkly pink dress, and I chose a simple, lacy tea-length gown in a pale gold that glimmered in the subdued lighting. Abby and I walked the short distance together, John insisting on including her in our ceremony. There hadn't been a dry eye in the house as he'd spoken of loving his two girls and being the man privileged to watch Abby grow.

We had celebrated hard. Eaten, drank, and danced the night away. Returned to the farm as husband and wife, John carrying me over the threshold. We had barely made it to our room before his suit and my pretty dress were on the floor.

I had been glad we hadn't planned to pick Abby up until later the next afternoon. We were delayed getting there, and I doubted anyone believed John's explanation of engine trouble.

Then we started our life together.

I still had the restaurant, but I also helped Helen run her wedding location. We offered delicious, local fare, made from the freshest ingredients. Handmade. Served by neighbors and friends.

The place was a roaring success, and it was booked solid for the next two years.

"What are you thinking about?"

I startled at John's voice, smiling as he walked toward me, a bouquet in his hand.

"Daydreaming. What are you doing here?"

"It's our anniversary. Did you think I forgot?"

I laughed. "You reminded me last week, last night, this morning as we made love, and you wrote me a poem. I knew you didn't forget."

"Well, I decided flowers were necessary."

I took the bouquet, inhaling the blooms' enticing scent. "Thank you."

He bent and kissed me. "Thank you for a wonderful first year. I look forward to many, many more."

Pulling out a chair, he sat beside me. "Memories," he murmured. "Such good memories."

"Yep. I was recalling how sexy you looked in your suit."

"Not half as sexy as you looked in that damn dress. I wanted to throw you over my shoulder and run someplace so I could rip it off you."

I nudged him. "What, my overalls don't do it for you?"

He tugged on my straps, pulling me close. "Woman, you do it for me all the time." He kissed me soundly. "Every. Damn. Day."

"I see."

"I got you a present," he murmured, still holding me close, his lips hovering near mine.

"Is it in your pocket, or you're just happy to see me?"

He started to laugh, kissing me again. "Both."

He pulled out a folded envelope. "It's not really from me, but I get to give it to you."

I took the envelope and unfolded the document in it, gasping in happiness. "Really? The building is mine?"

"Signed, sealed, and delivered."

I flung my arms around his neck. "I own a building!"

He hugged me close. "You do. The Dill has a permanent home, and if you want to expand, you can."

"I was thinking of putting a small market next door. Showcasing local goods."

He stroked my cheek. "Great idea. The tradesmen in town can help renovate it. Show off their skills. There is a new development down the road, seeing their work might help them find jobs."

"Perfect."

I smiled as I slipped my hand into my purse, pulling out a flat box. "I have something for you too."

"Yeah?"

I handed him the package. "Yeah. Happy anniversary, John."

He grinned. "I'm gonna love it."

"I hope so."

He unwrapped the box and pulled out a frame. He studied the blurry black-and-white image for a moment, then froze. He looked up, expectant and happy. "Really, Quinn?"

"I'm pregnant," I confirmed. I tapped the image. "That's our baby."

In seconds, I was in his arms, being cradled in his embrace. "When? How? Are you okay?"

"About eight weeks," I replied as he laid his hand on my stomach, his large palm pressed to me, his fingers spread wide. "I'm pretty sure you know how, and yes, I'm fine." I covered his hand. "I was tired last week, and it hit me that not only was I tired because we've been so busy, but I was late. I went to see the doctor two days ago." I sighed as I laid my head on his shoulder. "It's been all I could do not to tell you, but I knew you would love it as an anniversary gift."

He pressed a kiss to my head. "Best gift ever. But I'm coming to all the other appointments."

"Okay."

"Pumpkin is going to go wild." He chuckled. "So is Laura."

"I have to figure things out with the restaurant, here with Helen…" I trailed off.

"We will figure it all out," he assured me. "But right now, we're going to celebrate. Nothing else matters. You, me, Pumpkin, and baby." He was quiet for a moment. "Our family is growing, Quinn. Exactly the way I hoped."

I sighed, enjoying being in his arms.

"How about we go for a drive, pick up our girl, and take her for ice cream before we go out for dinner? We can tell her she is gonna be a big sister."

"Let's just stay home."

He chuckled, the sound reverberating through his chest. "Somehow I knew you'd say that. You always prefer to be home."

"I love home." I tilted up my head. "I love you."

He bent down, his mouth on mine. "I love you, darlin'. Happy anniversary."

A YEAR LATER -JOHN

A noise jolted me awake, and I slipped from the bed

before Quinn could. "I've got him," I assured her. "Go back to sleep."

I headed to the nursery, picking up our son, who instantly settled as I cradled him against my chest. After changing him, I went down the hall toward the kitchen, putting a bottle on to heat, then checked on Abby. She was fast asleep, her ceiling glowing with the stars we had put on it and her newly purple walls glittering softly. Pink was still good, but purple ruled. Add in glitter?

Abby was a happy girl.

I tugged her blanket up and bent to kiss her head. Then I carried my son back to the kitchen, checked the milk temperature, and sat in the large cuddle chair we had bought when Quinn was pregnant. She loved being held, and it was exactly what we needed on nights when she couldn't sleep and couldn't get comfortable in our bed.

I settled down and pressed the nipple to his mouth, smiling as he latched on fast. He made his growly noises as he sucked, and I watched him eat in wonder. At three months of age, he was still fascinating to me.

James Owen Elliott had come into the world two weeks late, screaming his displeasure and letting us know he had arrived and wanted our attention. Abby had promptly nicknamed him Jimjam, and it had stuck. Quinn had wanted to name him after me, but I thought another John was too much. James had been my gramps's name, and since it was my middle name, we both were happy.

Abby adored him, and no one could get him to quiet down when fussy the way his big sister could. He loved his momma fiercely, but he and I had a special bond. I loved the chance to sit in the dark and feed him. Talk to him about silly things. I told him stories of his grandparents, great-grandparents, and the farm. His aunt. His big sister. His amazing momma and how incredible she was. He listened, absorbing, I was certain, every single word. He was my boy.

I could hardly wait to get him on the tractor with me. Teach him about the fields and crops. Encourage him to discover the world. I wanted him to be free to choose the life he wanted, be it the land or an office. Or neither.

Abby was determined she was going to be a farmer like me. She loved every aspect of the land, and I loved teaching her. Whether her brother would remained to be seen.

If there would be more siblings was a mystery to be solved in the future.

Quinn appeared, smiling as she stood beside us, trailing a finger down his chubby cheek. "He's eating so well."

I grinned. "Like his daddy."

"He is certainly built like him."

Jimjam had been a large baby. Far bigger than Abby, which was the reason he might be the last of the line. Quinn was worried the next one might be even bigger.

"You know," I teased, "the next one could be a girl. A tiny one."

"Or a linebacker," Quinn responded.

"Three is a nice number."

She pursed her lips.

"Or four."

Her gaze snapped to mine, and I winked. "Simply saying. Any number up to five is good in my books."

Her eyes grew round with horror. "*John James Elliott.* You take that back."

I looked down at our son. "Momma isn't happy, little man. I need to go apologize."

She sniffed. "I know what your apology consists of. That's what got us into trouble in the first place. I'm not falling for that again."

I lifted him to my shoulder, rubbing his back. "I have no idea what you are referring to, Mrs. Elliott."

That made her smile. She loved it when I called her

Mrs. Elliott. I loved calling her that. "My wife" was a close second.

I held out my hand. "Come sit with us."

She snuggled beside me, resting her head on my shoulder as Jimjam burped, and I gave him back the bottle. He fell asleep while eating, his mouth going slack and a little dribble of milk leaking out. Quinn reached over, wiping it away with a sigh.

"He's so damn cute."

"He is."

"Maybe one more," she whispered.

"We can work on that."

"I want another girl."

"I'll do my best."

She looked up and I bent, kissing her. "We can always practice," I whispered.

She laughed, the sound low and sweet. "We don't need any practice, John. We're damn near perfect."

"Ah, but you know how I feel about anything less than an A-plus."

She stood. "Then you better be ready to show me your new tricks, Mr. Elliott. I'll try to judge fairly." She winked. "I'll be waiting. I hope you got enough sleep. You're gonna need it for what I have planned."

I watched her walk away, an extra swing to her hips. A smile tugged on my lips. I loved my wife. Our family. Our simple but incredible life. It was full of love, laughter, and joy. All because of her. She was the center of everything right in my world. She comforted me during bad times and was always the reason for the good times.

And she was full of shit.

I knew, without a doubt, she'd be out as soon as her head hit the pillow. And I would crawl in beside her, pull her into my arms and be content to fall asleep with her.

We'd wake early, hopefully before the baby, and greet the morning by making love, fast and furtive under the blankets. Or find five minutes together in the shower. A quick round on the sofa when the kids went to bed. Maybe a quickie at lunch if we were lucky.

Our all-nighters were a distant memory. At least for now.

I tucked our son back into bed, then headed to our room. As I suspected, my wife was asleep, her cheek cushioned on her hand, the moonlight showing me her form under the blankets.

I sighed as I slipped in beside her, and she eased back into my arms.

Tomorrow would come early, and the day would be another long one.

But as long as it ended the same way, her with me, it was good.

Simple as that.

Thank you so much for reading **A SIMPLE LIFE**. If you are so inclined, reviews are always welcome by me at your retailer.

If you love a growly hero, Richard and Katy VanRyan's story begins with my series The Contract. You meet an arrogant hero in Richard, which makes his story much sweeter when he falls.

If romantic comedy is your favorite trope, Liam and Shelby, from my novel Changing Roles, would be a recommended standalone to read next. It is a story of friends to lovers set in the bright lights of Hollywood.

Enjoy meeting other readers? Lots of fun, with upcoming book talk and giveaways! Check out Melanie Moreland's Minions on Facebook.

Join my newsletter for up-to-date news, sales, book

announcements and excerpts (no spam). Click here to sign up Melanie Moreland's newsletter or use the QR code below:

Scan To Sign Up Now

Visit my website www.melaniemoreland.com

Enjoy reading! Melanie

ACKNOWLEDGMENTS

To everyone on Team Moreland I am grateful and appreciate everything you do.

My Facebook reader group–Melanie's Minions—many thanks for your continued encouragement. Farmer John got his happily ever after thanks to your efforts.

To my hype team, the Author Agency team and book talkers—thank you for all your support.

Matthew—Always.

ALSO AVAILABLE FROM MORELAND BOOKS

Titles published under M. Moreland

Insta-Spark Collection

It Started with a Kiss

Christmas Sugar

An Instant Connection

An Unexpected Gift

Harvest of Love

An Unexpected Chance

Following Maggie

The Wish List

Wrapped In Love

Titles published under Melanie Moreland

The Contract Series

The Contract (Contract #1)

The Baby Clause (Contract Novella)

The Amendment (Contract #3)

The Addendum (Contract #4)

Vested Interest Series

BAM - The Beginning (Prequel)

Bentley (Vested Interest #1)

Aiden (Vested Interest #2)

Maddox (Vested Interest #3)

Reid (Vested Interest #4)

Van (Vested Interest #5)

Halton (Vested Interest #6)

Sandy (Vested Interest #7)

Vested Interest/ABC Crossover

A Merry Vested Wedding

ABC Corp Series

My Saving Grace (Vested Interest: ABC Corp #1)

Finding Ronan's Heart (Vested Interest: ABC Corp #2)

Loved By Liam (Vested Interest: ABC Corp #3)

Age of Ava (Vested Interest: ABC Corp #4)

Sunshine & Sammy (Vested Interest: ABC Corp #5)

Unscripted With Mila (Vested Interest: ABC Corp #6)

Men of Hidden Justice

The Boss

Second-In-Command

The Commander

The Watcher

The Specialist

Men of the Falls

Aldo

Roman

My Favorite

My Favorite Kidnapper

My Favorite Boss

Reynolds Restorations

Revved to the Maxx

Breaking The Speed Limit

Shifting Gears

Under The Radar

Full Throttle

Standalones

Into the Storm

Beneath the Scars

Over the Fence

The Image of You

Changing Roles

The Summer of Us

Happily Ever After Collection

Heart Strings

A Simple Life

ABOUT THE AUTHOR

NYT/WSJ/USAT international bestselling author Melanie Moreland, lives a happy and content life in a quiet area of Ontario with her beloved husband of thirty-plus years and their rescue cat, Amber. Nothing means more to her than her friends and family, and she cherishes every moment spent with them.

While seriously addicted to coffee, and highly challenged with all things computer-related and technical, she relishes baking, cooking, and trying new recipes for people to sample. She loves to throw dinner parties, and enjoys traveling, here and abroad, but finds coming home is always the best part of any trip.

Melanie loves stories, especially paired with a good wine, and enjoys skydiving (free falling over a fleck of dust) extreme snowboarding (falling down stairs) and piloting her own helicopter (tripping over her own feet.) She's learned happily ever afters, even bumpy ones, are all in how you tell the story.

Melanie is represented by Flavia Viotti at Bookcase Literary Agency. For any questions regarding subsidiary or translation rights please contact her at flavia@bookcaseagency.com

facebook.com/authormoreland

x.com/morelandmelanie

instagram.com/morelandmelanie

bookbub.com/authors/melanie-moreland

amazon.com/Melanie-Moreland/author/B00GV6LB00

goodreads.com/Melanie_Moreland

tiktok.com/@melaniemoreland

threads.net/@morelandmelanie

Made in the USA
Columbia, SC
20 February 2025